Meet the team:

Alex – A quiet lad from

the team in survival skills. His dad is in the SAS and Alex is determined to follow in his footsteps, whatever it takes. He who dares . . .

Li – Expert in martial arts and free-climbing, Li can get to grips with most situations . . .

Paulo – The laid-back Argentinian is a mechanical genius, and with his medical skills he can patch up injuries as well as motors . . .

Hex – An ace hacker, Hex is first rate at code-breaking and can bypass most security systems . . .

Amber – Her top navigational skills mean the team are rarely lost. Rarely lost for words either, rich-girl Amber can show some serious attitude . . .

With plenty of hard work and training, together they are Alpha Force – an elite squad of young people dedicated to combating injustice throughout the world.

In *Hostage* an extremely frosty reception awaits Alpha Force when they fly into Northern Canada . . .

www.kidsatrandomhouse.co.uk/alphaforce

Also available in the Alpha Force series:

SURVIVAL
RAT-CATCHER
DESERT PURSUIT
RED CENTRE

Coming soon:

HUNTED

HOSTAGE

RED
FOX

ALPHA FORCE: HOSTAGE

A RED FOX BOOK 0 09 943927 1

First published in Great Britain by Red Fox,
an imprint of Random House Children's Books, 2003

This edition published 2004

1 3 5 7 9 10 8 6 4 2

Papers used by Random House Children's Books are natural, recyclable products made from wood grown in sustainable forests. The manufacturing processes conform to the environmental regulations of the country of origin.

Typeset in Sabon by Palimpsest Book Production Limited,
Polmont, Stirlingshire

Red Fox Books are published by Random House Children's Books,
61–63 Uxbridge Road, London W5 5SA,
a division of The Random House Group Ltd,
in Australia by Random House Australia (Pty) Ltd,
20 Alfred Street, Milsons Point, Sydney, NSW 2061, Australia,
in New Zealand by Random House New Zealand Ltd,
18 Poland Road, Glenfield, Auckland 10, New Zealand,
and in South Africa by Random House (Pty) Ltd,
Endulini, 5A Jubilee Road, Parktown 2193, South Africa

THE RANDOM HOUSE GROUP Limited Reg. No. 954009
www.**kidsatrandomhouse**.co.uk

A CIP catalogue record for this book is available from the British Library.

Printed and bound in Great Britain by
Cox & Wyman Ltd, Reading, Berkshire

ALPHA FORCE

The field of operation...

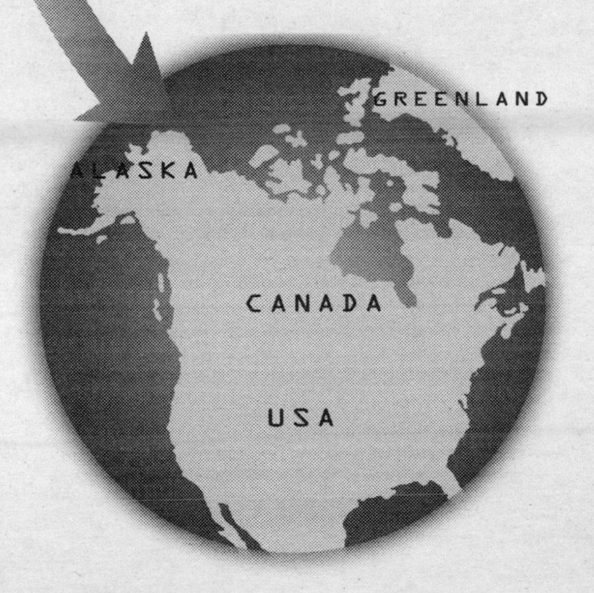

One

The polar bear floated in the dark water just under the ice-scattered surface of Hudson Bay. It was an old, one-eyed male with a set of four deep, jagged scars cutting through the empty eye socket and across its snout. The bear hung limply, swaying with the current. Its huge paws dangled lifelessly and loose folds of fur hung from its thin frame. It appeared to be dead, but an occasional silvery bubble rose from the corner of its jaw and its one eye was alert and watchful. Half-blinded and past its prime, this bear had learned how to be sly when stalking its prey.

Just ahead of the bear, a seaweed forest rose from the sea bed. A small group of arctic ringed seals was feeding and playing amongst the tall, swaying kelp stems and none of them had noticed the ghost-like shape floating on the edge of darkness. The bear was lean and hungry after a summer trapped on land and seals were its favourite food. They were sleek and fat with a thick, insulating layer of blubber that would help build up the bear's own fat reserves for the winter ahead. The bear watched the seals for a long time, carefully raising its snout above water every two minutes to take another lungful of air. It was choosing its target, looking for any sign of injury or slowness. Polar bears were strong swimmers but seals were much faster in the water and a surprise attack on the weakest individual was the bear's only chance.

The bear was not the only one watching the seals. Amber and Hex hung side by side in the icy water, totally unaware of the deadly hunter hovering behind them. It was late October in Hudson Bay and already temperatures in this north Canadian outpost on the edge of the Arctic Circle were well below freezing. Above their heads, irregular, ten-centimetre-thick sheets of sea ice were floating on the surface of the bay like scattered jigsaw pieces. By mid-winter, the jigsaw would be complete and a solid crust of ice up to three metres thick would cover the whole of Hudson Bay and the ocean beyond.

Even in October, an unprotected person diving beneath the ice would be dead from hypothermia within minutes, but Amber and Hex were each encased in three layers to insulate them against the killer cold. The outermost layer was a loose-fitting dry suit with moulded boots and latex wrist and neck seals. Under the suit, a second insulating layer of air was maintained by a low-pressure air hose attached at the chest. Finally, next to the skin, they each wore a complete covering of Thinsulate undergarments for extra warmth.

Amber's smile was wide behind her full face mask as she trained the beam of her underwater torch on the kelp forest. The seals were putting on a dazzling display of aquatics. At first the group had been wary, but Amber and Hex had left their underwater scooters on the sea bed and then waited patiently, treading water. Gradually, the seals had grown used to the torch beams lighting up their dim underwater world and had begun to hunt fish again. Now they were shooting back and forth through the beams of light like small, fat torpedoes, sometimes skimming past Amber and Hex with only centimetres to spare.

Amber looked over at Hex and he lowered his underwater camcorder and grinned back at her, his green eyes shining behind his mask. Hex was a Londoner and an expert hacker, a combination which meant that his natural habitat was most definitely indoors. When he was at home, he spent most of his free time surfing the Net or training at his local gym and the closest he got to nature was the occasional jog across Hampstead Heath. He had not been looking forward to this trip to the frozen wastes of northern Canada and the activity he had been dreading most was diving in sub-zero temperatures. To his surprise, he had discovered that he loved it.

Hex glanced down at his watch, checking the dive-time they had left. Alex, Li and Paulo, the other three members of Alpha Force, were waiting for them on the shores of Hudson Bay and Hex knew what would happen if he and Amber failed to return to base on time. He did not want the embarrassment of setting off a full search-and-rescue procedure simply because he had not kept an eye on the clock. The illuminated dial of his watch told him they could stay under for another ten minutes. Satisfied, Hex turned his attention back to Amber. He wriggled his gloved fingers and pointed down at his flippered feet, looking at her questioningly. She rolled her eyes at him. She knew what he was asking. Amber was a diabetic and diabetics can suffer from poor circulation, so it was particularly important that she did not allow her fingers and toes to get cold. Hex was her dive-buddy and dive-buddies were supposed to look out for each other, but in her opinion he was taking it a bit too far. This was the fourth time he had checked up on her. She tried ignoring him, but he simply stared, waiting for her answer. Finally, Amber scowled horribly and gave him a reluctant thumbs-up sign. Hex merely nodded an acknowledgement and turned back to filming the show. Amber tried to keep scowling but her wide smile returned as two seals whirled round her head once, twice, in a high-speed chase.

Anyone back at Amber's exclusive girls' boarding school in Boston, Massachusetts, would have been very surprised to see that smile. Since her parents had been killed in a plane crash a few years back, the tall, beautiful black American girl rarely smiled in a semester and preferred to be left alone. She had inherited billions of dollars from the software empire that her parents had built up, but the money did not ease her sadness. For a year after the death of her parents, Amber had stopped caring about her own life and that was a dangerous frame of mind for a diabetic. Several times that first year, her uncle, John Middleton, had been called out from New York when Amber had ended up in the hospital emergency ward after not bothering to check her blood sugar levels or inject her twice-daily dose of insulin.

Finally, a worried John Middleton had sent his niece to spend a few weeks on a sail-training ship as one of a crew of young people from all over the world. He was hoping that the experience might change Amber's outlook. What it did was force her into a life-or-death situation as she and the other four members of her watch team became marooned on an uninhabited island. As they struggled to survive, Amber, Li, Paulo, Hex and Alex, the five feuding members of A-Watch, had been forced to work together. By the time rescue arrived, they had formed themselves into a tight-knit team.

The team became Alpha Force after Amber discovered the truth about the death of her parents. The plane crash that killed her mother and father had not been an accident. It was deliberate sabotage. At first, Amber could not understand why anyone would want to murder her parents, but her uncle explained that they had become involved in some very dangerous undercover work after they started trying to put something back into a world that had given them so much. Posing as wealthy tourists, they had travelled to some of the world's poorest and most trouble-torn spots. There, they had slipped across borders into no-go areas such as war-zones or refugee camps, giving what help they could in situations where governments, aid agencies and environmental organizations were unable to intervene. Amber's uncle, John Middleton, had become their anchor man, organizing funds and equipment from his New York office, and together they had made a small difference. Medical supplies suddenly appeared in blockaded towns, secretly filmed footage exposing corrupt businesses or governments arrived at international news agencies, and war orphans were quietly smuggled across closed borders to start new lives elsewhere. As they became more effective, Amber's parents began to build up a list of powerful enemies and, somewhere along the line, one of those enemies disposed of them.

When Amber decided that she wanted to carry on the work of her parents, Alex, Li, Paulo and Hex had been right behind her and, with John Middleton as their anchor man, Alpha Force was born. Each of them had a special skill to bring to the team. Alex's father was in the SAS and had taught him how to stay alive in the most hostile environments. Li was a free climber and a martial arts expert. Paulo could drive just about anything and was also a skilled mechanic. Hex was a master hacker and code-breaker and Amber was their navigation expert.

Alpha Force had been working as an undercover unit for two years now, meeting up regularly for missions or training sessions. This time, the team had gathered in northern Canada for an exercise in cold-climate survival, and that was partly why Amber found it difficult to stop smiling. She was at her happiest when they were all together. Although she would never dream of telling the others, the fact was that Alpha Force, and Hex in particular, were now the people she loved most in the world.

Hex tapped her on the shoulder, making her jump. Amber wiped the smile from her face and scowled at him through her mask. It was a truly ferocious scowl, fierce enough to strip paint, but Hex did not even flinch. He was used to Amber. He stared back calmly, then pointed to his watch to show her that it was time to go. Reluctantly, Amber nodded.

Hex clipped the underwater camcorder to the belt at his waist, then turned slowly in the water until he was pointing towards the sea bed. He had learned early on that trying to do anything too quickly in a dry suit was not a good idea. Buoyancy control was the key to dry suit diving. The chest unit pumped air into the suit and an exhaust valve on the shoulder, which automatically let out any excess air, balanced this, but the remaining insulating layer could still cause problems to a novice diver. In two of his early dives, Hex had made the mistake of turning upside down too quickly. The air inside his suit had all migrated into his boots and he had suffered the indignity of floating helplessly up to the surface, feet first, with a laughing Amber waving goodbye from the sea bed.

Once Hex was sure he was not going to repeat his earlier performances, he grinned at Amber and kicked off with his flippers. To his relief, he glided gracefully down to the sea bed, where his underwater scooter was parked. Privately, he thought scooter was the wrong word for it. There were no handlebars or saddle, just a bright blue, propeller-driven cartridge that looked like a cartoon bomb. At least it was easy to control. Hex pointed it the way he wanted to go and then pressed down the two switches, one on each side of the handle. The scooter moved off, lighting up a cone-shaped slice of water ahead of it with its powerful headlights.

Amber started to follow Hex but could not resist turning back for one more look at the seals. A few seconds later she was once again absorbed in watching their antics. Hex had disappeared into the darkness, thinking she was right behind him. In the hostile waters of Hudson Bay, Amber had just made two deadly mistakes. She had lost sight of her dive-buddy and had stopped keeping a regular check on her surroundings.

The bear chose this moment to move in for the kill.

Amber blinked and stared hard at the kelp forest. The seals had disappeared. An instant earlier they had been right in front of her. Now the spaces between the seaweed strands were suddenly empty. Where had they gone? For three vital seconds, as the bear swam up behind her with steady strokes of its huge front paws, Amber stared stupidly at the kelp forest where the seals had been. When she finally realized that something must have scared them, it was too late. She turned in the water and came face to face with the bear.

Two

A massive bolt of shock ran through Amber as she saw the great scarred head just a few metres away. The bear lunged for her, opening its jaws wide, and Amber stared into the open mouth, taking in every detail of the ivory-yellow teeth, the purple gums and the long, bluish tongue. She screamed behind her mask and flung her hands up protectively as the bear prepared to crush her skull with one bite. She was still clutching the torch in one hand and that was what saved her. As her arms came up in front of her face, the torch beam shone into the bear's remaining eye, blinding it.

The bear pulled back, then lunged out and swiped at the torch with its paw. Its claws did not make contact with her hand but still Amber reeled from the power of the blow. The torch flew from her numb fingers and floated down to the sea bed, where it lay with the beam pointing upwards, floodlighting the scene.

There was an instant of stillness. The huge bear glared at Amber with its good eye, trying to decide whether this strange, elongated creature was food or threat. Amber stared back, frozen with fear. Up close, the size of the creature was overwhelming. It had to be three metres from nose to tail and its front paws were the size of small boulders. With a huge effort, Amber controlled her terror. Her brain started to work again and she realized that she was staring death in the face. A second later, her body jerked into action. She flipped over in the water and tried to swim for her scooter, but the air in her suit held her on a level with the bear.

Her frantic kicking stimulated the bear to attack again. It reared up in the water, reaching for her with its jaws wide and its claws ready. Amber stopped struggling to get away and prayed for a quick death, but the pain of ripping claws and crushing jaws never came. Instead, the bear jerked sideways as Hex came up on its blind side and rammed into its ribcage with his underwater scooter.

The bear tumbled away through the water with great bubbles of air exploding from its jaws and Hex went tumbling the other way, hanging grimly on to his scooter. He knew the machine was their only chance of escape. As soon as he could, he righted himself and pressed the buttons on the handle of the scooter, hoping the machine had not been too badly damaged by the impact. To his relief, the propeller started to turn and he was able to guide the scooter back to a dazed and terrified Amber.

The bear was heading for the surface, but Hex knew it would be back as soon as it had taken in another breath of air. Letting go of one side of the scooter, he grabbed Amber by the chin and turned her head towards him so that he could look into her eyes. She still had the dazed look of an animal expecting to die but, as soon as she focused on his face, her eyes sharpened. Hex put his arm round

Amber's waist and pulled her up against him so that they were both lying parallel behind the scooter. Amber was quick to understand his intention. She wrapped one arm around his waist in return and grabbed her side of the scooter with the other hand. Together, they each pressed one of the handle buttons and the scooter took off.

Hex looked back and felt his heart sink. The bear had replenished its air supply and was coming after them. It swam with slow, steady strokes of its front paws, holding its back legs stiffly like a rudder. Its black lips were pulled back from its teeth in a snarl and its one eye glared at them. Hex could see that the bear was in a killing rage and was not going to give up until it had caught them. He gritted his teeth and turned back to steering the scooter. The light grew brighter, which told him they were moving into shallower water, but their combined weight was dragging on the little machine. Even with them both helping it along by kicking their feet, the scooter moved forward at a speed which felt agonizingly slow to Hex. He looked behind him again. The bear was definitely gaining on them. Now he could see the scarring on its snout and each individual tooth in its gaping mouth. With a prickling of dread in his guts, Hex began to wonder whether they were going to make it.

On the shores of Hudson Bay, Paulo shivered as he gazed around the stark, grey and white landscape. In front of him, sheets of ice scraped and bumped together on the heaving water and behind him the flat, icy tundra stretched back to meet the tree line. Beyond that, a vast forest of spruce trees marched towards the horizon. The low sun gave even the smallest pebble a long shadow and the wind howled constantly, carrying with it an icy chill that came straight from the Arctic Circle.

'I am cold,' sighed Paulo mournfully. 'So very cold.'

Li put her mittened hands on her hips and looked the tall South American up and down. 'You can't possibly be cold,' she said. 'You have so many clothes on, you look like a very large snowball.' Her uptilted eyes creased into a smile. 'We all do,' she giggled, looking down at herself, then over to Alex.

All three of them were bundled up inside four

layers of arctic gear. It was standard military issue, so the colour was white, for camouflage in snow. Next to the skin, they were wearing thin cotton undergarments which were loose fitting and able to absorb any sweat the body produced. This was important when the temperature was well below zero. If the skin was kept dry, there would be no heat loss through sweat evaporation. Over the cotton undergarments they each wore a second layer made of tightly woven wool, with fastenings at the throat and wrists to prevent heat escaping. The third layer consisted of fleece-lined trousers and a hooded jacket and the final layer was another hooded jacket and trousers, this time padded with insulating material and with an outer covering that was both wind- and waterproof.

'I mean, I am cold in my soul,' said Paulo.

'Don't be such a drama queen,' said Li, punching him in the chest.

Paulo grinned down at her fondly. 'I miss the sun. I need the sun. I am like a big cat. A lion.'

'Yeah. You're grouchy, smelly and you sleep too much.'

'Back home in Argentina, it is warm,' continued Paulo, ignoring her insults. His brown eyes grew soft and distant as he pictured the sprawling buildings of his family cattle ranch. 'They will be sitting out on the veranda in only shirts and trousers. Not all this – stuff.' Paulo flipped the earflaps on his hat, then held out his mittened hands for Li to see. The mittens were attached to the sleeves of his coat with short lengths of cord. 'What am I? A baby?'

He looked so sorry for himself that Li reached out and gave him a hug.

Alex looked at them sideways and shook his head. 'If you lose a glove in northern Canada at this time of year, you'll soon be in big trouble. In these temperatures, you're risking frostbite. And if you touch anything metal with your bare hand, you're going to—'

'—lose all the flesh from our fingers,' said Li, crossing her eyes. 'We know. You told us.' She grinned at Alex, but he did not respond. Frowning, he turned back to scanning the surface of Hudson Bay.

'I'm bored,' announced Li. 'We need some action

around here.' She had completed her last dive of the day less than an hour earlier and already she was itching to do something else. Li was incredibly fit from years of free climbing and martial arts training and she always had lots of energy to burn. She could not tolerate inactivity for long, which meant she often got into trouble jumping into situations without thinking first. Now she sighed and bounced up and down on the spot. 'Do we have to wait much longer?' she demanded.

'They should be back by now,' muttered Alex, his grey eyes cloudy with worry as he searched the bay for any sign of Amber and Hex.

Paulo fought his way through layers of clothing to check his wristwatch. 'But they are only one minute late,' he said.

'A minute is a long time if you're trapped somewhere with your air running out,' snapped Alex.

Li and Paulo looked at one another, then moved up to stand on either side of Alex. 'We will all look,' said Paulo quietly.

'They'll turn up any second now,' added Li.

There was a moment of uneasy silence as they all

stood together on the viewing platform at the back of the tundra buggy, scanning the bay. The tundra buggy was a square, metal-sheathed truck which sat high above the ground on huge tyres. The Hudson Bay area was home to hundreds of polar bears, especially at this time of the year when they returned to the coast, eager to hunt seals again after a summer trapped on land. Tempers frayed as the bears waited hungrily for the sea ice to become strong enough to hold their weight, and so the armoured tundra buggy had been built to withstand the most ferocious bear attack. As well as being a means of safe transport, crawling slowly across the icy, rock-strewn ground on its huge tyres, the truck could also serve as a bunkhouse big enough for a small group to live in. The metal body was well insulated and foldaway bunks had been built into the walls.

Suddenly, Li pointed to a spot just offshore. 'There they are!' she yelled.

Alex followed her pointing finger and saw Amber and Hex emerging from the water. He let out a breath he had not realized he was holding and pushed his fair hair back out of his eyes. 'Those two need to learn how to tell the time properly,' he said, easing the knots out of his shoulders.

'Wait,' said Paulo. 'Something is not right.'

Alex looked again at Amber and Hex. They had left the scooter rolling in the surf and were powering towards the shore, pushing plates of ice out of their way. As they waded, they ripped off their masks and tore at the harnesses strapping the heavy air cylinders to their backs. Even from this distance, the terror on their faces was horrifyingly clear.

'What's wrong with them?' asked Li. 'Why do they keep looking back?'

Paulo searched the water behind Amber and Hex and spotted a V-shaped wake heading right for them. 'Something is chasing them!' he shouted, pointing to the wake.

Amber and Hex reached the shallows and hopped and stumbled towards the shore, yanking their flippers off as they went. They began to run towards the tundra buggy, dropping their air cylinders on to the frozen ground with a clang that echoed round the bay.

'Put the ladder out!' yelled Hex. 'The ladder!'

Paulo and Li sprang into action, lifting a short aluminium ladder over the side of the truck. There were hooks at the top of the ladder, which slotted over the handrail that ran around the sides of the viewing platform. The hooks held the ladder in place, with the bottom rung hanging a metre and a half above the ground. Meanwhile, Alex watched the V-shaped wake until the thing that was making it began to emerge from the water.

'Bear,' he breathed as the triangular head came into view.

THREE

As soon as the bear's snout was above water, it opened its jaws and roared a challenge. Amber screamed and pushed herself to run faster. Hex twisted to look over his shoulder as he ran. His foot caught on a boulder and he fell full-length on the frozen ground. Amber continued for a few more paces before she realized that Hex was no longer with her. She turned and ran back to him as the bear splashed out on to the shore.

'C'mon! C'mon!' she screamed, grabbing Hex by the arm and hauling him to his feet. Together they staggered on towards the tundra buggy as the bear broke into a pigeon-toed lope behind them. Its low shoulders swung back and forth and its claws gouged the frozen snow as it picked up speed.

Up on the viewing platform, Paulo and Li hung over the handrail, ready to grab Amber and Hex and haul them up to safety. They were both screaming encouragement. Amber and Hex put on a burst of speed, but the bear was bounding now, charging after them with distance-eating strides. Despite its huge bulk, it was capable of dangerous speeds over short distances. When stalking a seal on land, a bear will use stealth to get as close as possible to its prey before going into a final charge that can be as fast as twenty-five miles an hour.

'They're not going to make it,' yelled Li. 'We have to do something!'

Alex suddenly turned and slammed open the door to the living quarters of the buggy. He had remembered the tranquillizer gun hanging on the wall inside. Seconds later, he skidded out on to the platform again, carrying a long, slim rifle with a telescopic sight. A tranquillizer dart was already in place in the barrel. Alex steadied his arm against the handrail and took aim. He got the bear in his sights but Amber and Hex were directly between him and his target. He could not get a clear shot.

'Shoot now!' yelled Paulo. 'You must shoot now!'

Alex cursed and moved into the far corner of the viewing platform, but still he could not get a clear shot.

Hex and Amber reached the tundra buggy together. Hex grabbed Amber round the hips and boosted her up on to the bottom rung of the ladder. She climbed up as best she could but the wet rubber of her suit kept slipping on the rungs. Paulo and Li leaned down as far as they could and grabbed her under the arms. They hauled her over the side and on to the floor of the viewing platform.

'Hex!' she sobbed, scrambling to her feet as the bear roared again directly below them.

Hex leaped for the ladder, caught the bottom rung and started to climb. His foot slipped and he fell back to the ground. The bear was nearly on him. Desperately he scrambled to his feet again, grabbed the bottom rung and swung his legs up out of the way as the bear pounced on the patch of snow where he had been a split second earlier. It brought its massive forepaws down so hard, the frozen surface cracked into hundreds of pieces and burst upwards in a white explosion.

Hex hung on to the ladder just above the bear's jaws. His feet were hooked around the fourth rung and his gloved hands clung to the bottom rung. With a dull horror, he realized that not only could he go no further, he was slowly losing his grip on the rungs. Below him the bear was still raking through the snow, but soon it would look up and see him hanging there like a fruit waiting to be picked. Hex closed his eyes.

'Paulo! Grab my legs!' yelled Li. She dived over the viewing platform wall so quickly, Paulo barely had time to get a grip on her. Li slammed into the ladder with a grunt and clamped her strong, climber's hands around Hex's ankles. The bear looked up, then raised its front paw, preparing to smash Hex off the ladder.

'Pull!' yelled Li.

Alex dropped the rifle and joined Paulo and Amber

as they yanked the combined weight of Li and Hex upwards. Hex let go of the bottom rung and swung his arms up out of the way just as the bear tried to knock him to the ground. He had a nightmare close-up of the beast's jaws snapping shut centimetres from his nose. A blast of hot, stinking breath exploded into his face before he was pulled up to the safety of the viewing platform.

For a few seconds they all lay in a stunned heap on the floor of the platform. Hex sucked air in through his nose and caught the fishy, rotting stench of the old bear's breath in his nostrils. He retched once and then again before he managed to get control of his stomach. 'That bear badly needs a Tic-tac,' he said weakly.

Suddenly the tundra buggy lurched violently as the bear slammed into the back of it. Then, with a screeching of metal, the handrail around the platform began to bend. The bear had hooked its claws around one of the higher rungs and was pulling down on the ladder with all its considerable weight. Even an average-sized adult male could weigh as much as six fully-grown men and this bear was a monster.

'Can they climb?' asked Paulo, looking at Li.

'They can climb trees,' said Li.

'What about ladders?' asked Paulo.

Li shrugged, then flinched as the bear slammed into the back of the tundra buggy again.

'Stay down,' said Alex. He scrambled to his feet and picked up the rifle. Carefully, he leaned over the side of the platform and raised the gun but he did not fire immediately. Instead, he waited for the bear to see the weapon. He knew that most of the bears in Hudson Bay had been tranquillized and tagged at one time or another. It followed that they must associate the weapon with a certain amount of pain and fear. This bear might just retreat at the sight of the tranquillizer rifle.

The bear turned its head and glared at Alex with its good eye. Its ears flattened when it caught sight of the rifle. Slowly it let go of the ladder and went down on to all fours. It huffed a few times, then yawned as a sign of appeasement and looked away. Alex grinned. His plan seemed to be working. A few seconds later the bear moved off at a steady lope, heading inland and looking back over its shoulder every now and then. Alex kept the rifle trained on the bear until, finally, it disappeared from view.

'Was that enough action for you, Li?' asked Alex, twenty minutes later.

They were gathered in the living area of the tundra buggy. Amber and Hex had changed out of their diving gear and were sitting with their hands wrapped around cups of hot soup. The vehicle heaters were on full but an occasional shiver still trembled through Amber's body.

'Blood sugar check,' said Hex briefly, watching Amber shudder.

She nodded meekly and reached for the pouch at her belt which contained her insulin injection pens and blood-sugar testing kit. Hex blinked with surprise. Normally, Amber hated being told what to do and he had expected an argument, but the encounter with the bear seemed to have knocked all the fight out of her.

'That bear was Cyclops,' said Li, watching as Amber pricked her finger and pressed it to the end of a thin plastic strip. 'The bad-tempered one Papaluk was telling us about – remember? I recognized him from his mug shot in her record book. One eye and four scars across the snout.'

Papaluk was an environmental scientist working in the Hudson Bay area. She and Li's zoologist parents had worked together on a conservation project in India and she had remained a close family friend ever since. Li had arranged for Alpha Force to stay with Papaluk while they carried out their cold-climate training. The cover story was that Li and her friends were into extreme sports and, after some initial misgivings about their safety, Papaluk had accepted that they knew what they were doing and had left them to it.

'We should take the tundra buggy back and warn Papaluk that he's in the area and acting meaner than ever,' said Li.

'We're due to finish here now, anyway,' said Alex, glancing at his watch. 'If we're going inland today, we need to get moving. We don't want to be setting up camp in the dark.'

This was their last morning on the coast. After the diving, they were planning to say their goodbyes to

Papaluk before heading inland on snowmobiles for a few days of survival training.

'Are you up to it?' asked Hex, watching Amber check the digital reading which measured her blood sugar level.

'I will be,' said Amber, pulling an insulin pen from the pouch. 'Soon as I stick myself with this.' She lifted her top, pinched up a fold of skin on her stomach and pressed the pen to it. One click and the pen delivered a pre-set dose of insulin. 'All done,' she said, packing the pen away into her belt pouch.

'Let us go then,' said Paulo, clambering into the driving seat. He started the engine and eased the big vehicle into gear. Slowly, the tundra buggy lumbered off over the rocky ground, heading for Papaluk's observation cabin on the other side of the headland.

Four

In the cabin, Papaluk sat at her workbench, checking through the e-mail that she was about to send. Her laptop was surrounded by an untidy jumble of scientific equipment, scribbled research notes and dirty crockery. In the ten years since she had graduated, she had worked in exotic locations all over the world, but when she was offered this research post just below the Arctic Circle in the far north of Canada, she had jumped at the chance. All her friends thought she was crazy, choosing to work in one of the coldest places on Earth, but Papaluk was a Canadian Inuit and she felt perfectly at home in the vast, icy wildernesses of Hudson Bay.

One of her jobs was to keep a check on the large population of polar bears roaming the bay area. The tundra buggy kept her safe when she was outside and, to keep her safe inside, the observation cabin where she lived and worked had been set on top of an eighteen-metre-high tower. The tower had four steel legs, with a strengthening network of horizontal support struts. A ladder, enclosed in protective ribs of steel, climbed up to the small viewing platform at the front of the cabin. Steel hawsers stretched from the top of the tower to the frozen ground, anchoring the cabin and making the structure strong enough to withstand 100 m.p.h. winds.

The observation cabin was the only building in this part of Hudson Bay. Perched high above the frozen ground like an oversized bird table, it commanded stunning views across the bay, the wide tundra and the great forest beyond. On clear winter nights, Papaluk liked to sit out on the viewing platform in her sleeping bag, waiting for a glimpse of the aurora borealis, or northern lights. On a good night, the dazzling light display would go on for hours and the sky would be filled with dancing ribbons of colour so beautiful it brought tears to her eyes. The northern lights held a special place in Papaluk's heart. Her mother had died a few years back and she still missed her. Traditionally, the Inuit believed that the colours were spirit torches sent to guide the dead home to a land of light lying beyond the dark shell of the sky. Papaluk liked to imagine that her mother was up there, watching over her and waiting to guide her home when the time came.

Papaluk loved her cabin. The well-insulated walls made it warm and cosy, even when the wind was strong enough to make the steel support hawsers sing. Sometimes the whole structure swayed in the wind like a ship at sea, but she always felt safe and protected inside.

Until now.

Papaluk's broad cheekbones were flushed with anxiety as she checked through the e-mail she had just written. Her hand shook as it hovered over the mouse button. She hesitated, then withdrew her hand and turned from the laptop to check through her notes one more time. There it was in black and white. The test results showed that cyanide waste was being dumped illegally into one of the rivers flowing into Hudson Bay.

She had first begun to suspect something six months earlier, when she had detected an unusually high number of miscarriages and birth deformities amongst the bear and seal populations in the bay. Since then, she had seen an increasing number of fish-eating birds and animals showing signs of cyanide poisoning, but she had been unable to find concrete evidence until Li and her friends had turned up with their cold-water diving gear. Earlier in the week they had collected specimens of water, plants and dead or dying fish from the mouth of the river for her and she had finally been able to carry out the necessary tests.

Cyanide was used in the gold-mining industry and there was a gold mine on the banks of the river, fifty miles inland. Papaluk knew that the mine had been failing, but an American-based corporation had taken it over the previous year, sacking all the local workers and bringing in their own men. The new company was secretive about its mining methods, but Papaluk had investigated on the Net and discovered that the mine was now making a profit for the first time in years.

Earlier that morning Papaluk had contacted the mine's management. As she expected, they had denied any illegal dumping of cyanide waste and she had explained that they left her with no alternative but to make her findings public. She had spent the rest of the morning putting her evidence together. Now she was ready. One click of the mouse and her e-mail would be sent to every government and environmental agency in Canada and North America. The reason for her hesitation was that she knew she was about to make a very powerful enemy. Daniel Usher was the head of the company that had bought the mine and he had a reputation for ruthlessness.

As Papaluk scanned the e-mail once more, she heard the mosquito whine of an approaching snowmobile. Like most Inuit, Papaluk was very sociable. She reckoned that if someone was prepared to travel through sub-zero temperatures to pay her a visit, then the least she could do was to give them a warm welcome. Normally, she would have rushed out on to the platform of her observation cabin to see who had come to call, but she was so involved in what she was doing, she did not even raise her head.

The mosquito whine stopped as the snowmobile came to a halt on the hard-packed snow below the observation hut. Still, Papaluk did not move. It was the custom for unexpected visitors to call out from the bottom of the tower, so when she heard the clang of booted feet climbing up the ladder without being invited, she presumed that Li and the others had returned. The climber had nearly reached the top of the tower when Papaluk remembered two things. One, Li and her friends were travelling by tundra buggy. Two, they were all wearing mukluks, soft boots with a rubber sole. This visitor had arrived by snowmobile and the boots she could hear clanging against the ladder rungs had hard soles.

An icy chill of fear ran down her spine. She turned on her stool to see a black silhouette clambering on to the viewing platform outside the cabin. It was a man, a big man, and suddenly Papaluk knew in her gut that he was not friendly. Surging to her feet, she ran for the door. There was an old-fashioned bolt under the handle which she never normally bothered to use. If she could just lock the door, it would buy her a few minutes to call for help on her phone. She fumbled to grasp the bolt and slide it across, but she was trying too hard and her fingers kept slipping. The man was on the platform now. Two strides and he would be at the door. Papaluk whimpered in fear and frustration. She finally managed to get a firm grip on the bolt handle. With a sigh of relief, she yanked hard. The bolt was stiff with disuse and refused to move.

The man ran at the door and rammed it with his shoulder. It smashed open and knocked her sprawling. She scrambled to her feet, grabbed the heavy microscope from her workbench and raised it above her head, preparing to hit the intruder. The man stopped, spread his arms wide and smiled. It was the smile that made Papaluk hesitate. Had she got it wrong? Was this a friendly visit after all? The man's smile widened. He had an honest, open face and his bright blue eyes gleamed with amusement.

Papaluk lowered the microscope and tried a tentative smile of her own. Quick as a snake, the man slammed his fist into her stomach. She dropped the microscope and doubled over. The pain made her eyes stream with tears and a high, whooping noise came out of her mouth as she tried to find some air. With a great effort, she raised her head and saw the logo on the man's padded jacket. It said USHER MINING CORPORATION.

Suddenly Papaluk knew what she had to do. Half-straightening, she turned to her workbench, pretending to clutch the edge of the bench for support. She reached out a shaking hand towards the mouse but, before she could click the button to send the e-mail, the man grabbed her by the hair and yanked her away from the bench. Papaluk screamed in pain and clawed at the man's hand. He let her go and she fell to the floor, clutching her head. Calmly, the man leaned over and deleted the e-mail, then severed the Internet connection. He picked up her notes, folded them and stuffed them inside his jacket, then he checked the workbench for any other evidence. Satisfied, he grabbed a glass sample jar and smiled down at Papaluk.

'Come along,' he said.

'Wh-where are we going?'

'Not far.'

The man was very strong. Within a few minutes, despite all her struggles, he had bundled her into her outdoor clothes and was forcing her down the ladder ahead of him. She reached the ground and started to run, but he was on her within two steps.

'You have guests?' he asked, turning her to face the line of snowmobiles and loaded trailers that were waiting for Alpha Force to return.

'They're only kids!' cried Papaluk. 'And they don't know anything!'

'When will they be back?'

'Not for a few days,' said Papaluk hastily, but she could not help glancing along the shore to make sure there was no sign of an approaching tundra buggy.

'That soon?' said the man, catching her glance. 'We'd better get on with it.'

Holding her upper arm in a vice-like grip, he frogmarched her down to the water. When she realized what he was going to do, Papaluk began to cry and her tears made frozen, white trails on her cheeks.

'Please . . . Please don't. I won't tell anyone about the cyanide. I promise,' she begged.

The man shook his head sadly. 'Sorry,' he said. 'You know how it is. Boss's orders.'

'Then let me talk to him!' cried Papaluk as they reached the water line. 'We can go back to the cabin and call him. I'm sure, if I talk to him—'

Her words were cut off as the man suddenly took her by the shoulders and threw her down into the icy waters of Hudson Bay. The cold was so intense it made all her muscles go into instant spasm. Her mouth opened wide and water flooded into her throat and lungs. She swallowed convulsively and the water entered her stomach, drastically reducing her core body temperature. Papaluk curled into a ball under the water as her muscles contracted even further. It was as though she had received a massive electric shock. The man was holding her down under the water but there was no need. The pain of the muscle cramps was overwhelming and she could not struggle.

Just as she thought she was going to drown, the man hauled her back out of the water and up on to the ice-covered shore. Papaluk lay curled where he had dropped her, shuddering with intense muscle cramps and coughing up water. She knew she had to get back to the warmth of the cabin. If she stayed out in this wind in soaking wet clothes the heat would drain out of her at a catastrophic rate and she would be dead within minutes. She held out a shaking hand to the man but he simply stood and watched her with a mildly interested look on his face. Papaluk turned on to her front and tried to push herself up off the ground but the man planted a foot on the back of her neck and held her down. Papaluk whimpered once, then concentrated on trying to strip off her soaking clothes, but her hands had contracted into claws and she could not get a grip. As her struggles weakened, the man removed his foot from the back of her neck and stood back, watching. Papaluk began to drag herself towards the cabin but her claw hands could not find a purchase on the ice and she did not get far. The rough surface tore her fingers to shreds but she was so numb with cold, she could not feel it. For five long minutes she struggled to save herself until her core body temperature dropped to a critical level. Gradually, her feet stopped kicking and her hands grew still. Her muscles relaxed and she lay quiet on the ice, barely conscious and breathing shallowly. The man watched her for a moment longer, then bent forward and placed the glass specimen jar next to her hand. If anyone found the body before the bears disposed of it, they would think she had fallen in as she tried to collect a water sample.

'A tragic accident,' he whispered, easing a strand of frozen hair away from her cheek before turning and walking away.

Papaluk was not cold any more, even though her hair and clothes were now sheathed in ice. The signals from her nerve endings were no longer getting through and all her major organs were slowly shutting down. The surfaces of her lungs had frozen and the cells in her oxygen-starved brain were winking out one by one. A film of clear ice formed over her open eyes, acting like a prism and breaking the light into glowing ribbons of colour. She was face down on the snow, but she thought she was looking at the sky. She thought the northern lights were dancing in her eyes and her mother had come to take her home.

Papaluk smiled as she died.

FIVE

Paulo brought the tundra buggy to a gentle halt beside Papaluk's tower. After a quick check for bears, Amber and Li opened up the back of the buggy and lowered the ladder. Paulo, Hex and Alex formed a passing line between the tundra buggy and the snowmobiles and Amber and Li handed down all the diving equipment. They did this in synchronized silence. They had been working together for so long now that there was no need for talking. During their trip inland, Alpha Force were planning on making some dives under the frozen surface of one of the lakes, which was why they were packing the diving equipment into one of the snowmobile trailers. The other trailers were already packed with equipment and supplies, ready for the trip.

Paulo smiled as he patted the nose of his snowmobile. It had been fun driving the tundra buggy, but he was looking forward to some extreme riding in the snowy forests of the interior. They would have to be on the look-out for polar bears to start with, but once they were away from the coast the snowmobiles would be safe enough.

At the last minute, Alex added the tranquillizer rifle to the trailer. Papaluk would not need it. She had another one propped by the door of her cabin. 'Right,' he said, securing the cover over the trailer. 'We're ready to head out.'

A fizz of excitement coursed through him as he spoke. The week of diving and bear-watching with Papaluk had been fine, but there had been no real challenge to it. He, Paulo and Hex had slept in comfort on padded bunks in the tundra buggy, and Li and Amber had shared the cabin with Papaluk. There had been hot meals waiting for them at the end of each day and the cabin was packed with all the latest communications technology, including satellite television reception. Alex had found it slightly strange, watching cookery and make-over programmes in the middle of the Canadian wilderness. He much preferred to be out there, depending on his own expertise and instincts for survival, which was why he was looking forward to this second leg of the exercise.

'I'll just let Papaluk know about the return of Cyclops,' said Li.

'Where is Papaluk, anyhow?' asked Amber, gazing up at the cabin. 'She usually comes out to say hi.'

For the first time, Alpha Force became aware of the silence. At this time of the day Papaluk usually took a break from her work, brewed up a fresh pot of coffee and played a CD of her favourite band, very loudly. Today there was no smell of coffee and no music blasting out over the tundra, only the howling of the wind.

'Maybe she's still trying to sort out those cyanide-dumpers,' said Hex, looking up at the cabin.

They had all been aware of how distracted Papaluk had been at breakfast. She had collected all the evidence she needed, but still she had not been looking forward to taking on the might of Usher Mining Corporation.

'I'll go and see how she's doing,' said Li, jumping on to the tower ladder. She sprinted up the narrow rungs as though she was running up a flight of stairs, then hopped up on to the viewing platform and disappeared from sight.

A minute later, she was back, hanging over the viewing platform rail with a puzzled look on her face. 'She's not here,' she said.

Alpha Force looked at one another uneasily.

'Then where is she?' demanded Amber, her voice high with anxiety.

'She cannot have gone far,' said Paulo. 'Not without the tundra buggy.'

On the viewing platform, Li suddenly straightened up. 'Oh no,' she gasped, pointing out towards the bay. 'Down there by the shoreline.'

The other four looked but could see nothing from their lower perspective.

'What is it?' asked Alex, but the chill in his guts told him he already knew.

'It's Papaluk,' quavered Li. 'And she's not moving.'

They raced down to the water and gathered round Papaluk's still body. She was lying face down so they eased her over on to her back. As they moved the body, the layer of ice covering her clothes and hair crackled and splintered. Paulo kneeled beside her head and pressed his fingers to the pulse point on the side of her neck. After a few minutes he shook his head. No-one argued with him. It was obvious that Papaluk was dead.

'She's smiling,' breathed Amber.

They were all quiet for a moment, staring transfixed at Papaluk's face. She looked like an ice princess. Each lash fringing her dark, slanted eyes was white with frost. Her face sparkled as though it was encrusted with tiny diamonds and her hair was spiked with icicles.

'What happened?' asked Li, her voice shaking with shock.

'I think maybe she slipped and fell in while she was taking a water sample,' said Paulo, nudging the sample jar with his toe.

'Yeah, but she got herself out again,' said Amber.

'Why couldn't she get back to the cabin?'

'She wouldn't've had much chance in these temperatures,' said Alex. 'You lose heat twenty-five times faster when your clothes are soaked through.'

'That's not how it was,' said Hex slowly. They all turned to look at him. Hex was the code-breaker and puzzle-solver of the group. If there was something wrong with a scenario, he always spotted it. Now, his green eyes were sharp as he looked down at Papaluk's body, then lifted his head to scan the bay. 'That's how we're meant to think it was,' he added grimly. 'But that's not how it happened. This is . . . wrong.'

'Tell us,' said Alex.

'Papaluk had no need to be down here. We'd collected all her samples for her. And even if she had decided to get just one more, this is still all wrong.'

'What is wrong?' asked Paulo.

'The sample jar. It's next to her hand. With the lid screwed on.' Hex sighed with annoyance at their puzzled expressions. 'Are we really supposed to believe that she leaned over to collect a sample, fell in, then managed to haul herself back out again, still holding on to the jar?'

'You're right,' said Alex. 'She would've let go of it. It should be at the bottom of the bay.'

'And once she climbed out of the water, did she really spend precious time finding the jar top and making sure it was screwed back on before she died? No. I think someone tried to make this look like an accident,' said Hex, scanning the bay again. He unslung the underwater camcorder from his shoulder and began filming the scene.

Li frowned. She was not sure she liked Hex filming her friend's dead body. When she was alive, Papaluk had always put her hand over the lens when Hex pointed the camcorder at her, but she could not do that now. 'What are you doing?' asked Li.

'Evidence,' said Hex briefly.

Li was about to object, but stopped with her hand raised and her mouth open as the tones of a mobile phone suddenly rang out across the bay. They were coming from somewhere near the cabin. Alpha Force tensed and slowly turned round. The ring tones stopped, cut off in mid-trill, and a tall, blond man stood up behind a large rock. He held a mobile phone in his hand. He had obviously just fumbled it from his pocket and turned it off. He waved and smiled at them, then disappeared behind the rock. An engine coughed into life and the man emerged again, riding a snowmobile. He drove slowly towards them, still smiling.

Everyone looked from the man to one another, trying to make sense of this strange appearance. Only Hex did not seem confused. He turned the camcorder on to the man and carried on filming. The man's easy smile wavered for a second, then settled back into place. Hex used the camcorder lens to zoom in on the logo on the man's jacket. It said USHER MINING CORPORATION.

Hex nodded. It was what he had expected to see. 'Run,' he said flatly.

'Excuse me?' said Paulo.

'We have to run. Head for the snowmobiles. Now!'

Hex's final shout jolted the other four into action. They took off, sprinting across the packed snow, but the man was faster. He revved the snowmobile engine and brought the machine round in a skidding turn across their path, spattering them with sharp needles of ice. They stumbled to a halt, covering their eyes against the flying ice slivers. When they lowered their hands again, the twin barrels of a sawn-off shotgun were trained on Hex's chest.

The man was not smiling now. He climbed down from his snowmobile, keeping the shotgun trained steadily on Hex. 'Give me the camcorder,' he ordered.

'Come and get it,' said Hex, still filming.

In reply, the man pumped the shotgun with a loud, double click, pushing a cartridge into the chamber.

'So, just for the camera,' said Hex steadily. 'You're the man who murdered our friend Papaluk.'

The man raised the gun to his shoulder again.

'You work for Usher Mining Corporation and your name is . . . ?'

'Shut up,' said the man. A muscle was twitching in his jaw and his hands tightened on the shotgun.

'Your company has been dumping cyanide waste into the river to avoid reclamation and water treatment costs,' continued Hex. 'And Papaluk found out about it, didn't she? So you killed her. And now you're going to shoot me.'

The man scowled and took a step towards Hex.

'Hex, you idiot!' yelled Amber. 'Give the guy what he wants!'

The man was distracted by Amber's sudden shout. It was only for an instant but that was all the time Li needed. While the man's head was turned towards Amber, Li launched herself high into the air with one leg held out stiffly in front of her. Her foot slammed into the side of his face with a dull thud. Li was wearing the soft mukluks, but all her skill and fury at the murder of Papaluk went into the kick and they all heard the snap as the man's cheekbone broke.

With a roar of pain, he staggered backwards and sat down hard on the snow, still clutching the shotgun. Li came down lightly on her feet and turned, bouncing on her toes and ready to attack again. Her face was still twisted with anger.

Hex assessed her chances and decided they were not good enough. The man might be down and injured but he still had possession of a sawn-off shotgun. Hex grabbed Li by the arm and shook his head. The man in the snow came up onto his knees.

'Run!' yelled Amber.

Alpha Force needed no second telling. They were off and running towards their snowmobiles while the man was still kneeling and waiting for his head to clear. They were running against the wind and all the layers of clothing they were wearing made it difficult to move fast. The skin tightened between their shoulder blades as they ran. With every second that passed, they were expecting a shotgun blast to ring out behind them.

Finally, they reached the line of snowmobiles parked at the base of the tower.

'Fan out!' yelled Alex as he flung himself into the saddle. 'And head for the tree line! We need some cover!'

The keys were in the ignition and, in a matter of seconds, they were revving their engines. The machines leaped forward and they headed towards the trees, fanning out until they were spread out in a long line across the snow.

Behind them, the man staggered to his feet, clutching the rifle in one hand and his cheek in the other. Bracing his knees, he steadied himself and raised the shotgun to his shoulder. The sawn-off barrels jerked from one white-clad, hooded rider to the next, searching for the one carrying the camcorder, but the man could not tell which one was Hex and they were getting further away by the second. With a curse, he reached over his shoulder and pushed the shotgun into the holster on his back. Then, clutching his cheek, he hurried over to his snowmobile and set off in pursuit.

Six

'Faster!' yelled Paulo, glancing behind him as the shrill engine note of the man's snowmobile started up. The tree line was still at least five minutes' hard riding away and their pursuer would stop at nothing to get hold of the incriminating camcorder evidence. Paulo took the lead, pushing his snowmobile up to breakneck speed. The frozen surface was dangerously uneven in places, but he did not slacken his pace. Instead, he simply rode his bucking machine over the rutted snow, clinging on like a cowboy at a rodeo and ignoring the scream from the overheated engine. The others fell into line behind him, picking up their speed too.

It was a nightmarish race. The snowmobiles were being pushed to their limit. The skis on the fronts of the little machines were twisting and jerking crazily and the belts on the rear caterpillar tracks were in danger of coming off their wheels. Alpha Force were all fully dressed for travelling and their hoods were securely tied, but the goggles they used when riding the snowmobiles were still swinging from the handlebars. The icy wind was cutting into their exposed cheeks and noses like a knife and tears were streaming from the corners of their eyes.

Halfway to the tree line, black smoke began to pour from the back of Alex's machine but he gritted his teeth and kept the engine at full throttle. He could not afford to slow down. Alpha Force had a head start on their pursuer, but the man was travelling light, with no trailer to pull, and he was slowly gaining on them.

By the time they reached the trees, the man was less than a minute behind. Paulo slewed his machine to the right in a tight turn, sending up a huge fan of snow. He rode along the edge of the stand of spruce trees until he found a track, then he swung the snowmobile in between the trees and the other four followed him.

It was a mixed blessing to be in amongst the spruces. The wind was suddenly gone, giving their smarting cheeks and streaming eyes a chance to recover, but the snow was much deeper here, which put more of a strain on the snowmobiles. The danger of smashing into a tree or being knocked from their machines by a low branch meant that they had to slow right down and that felt bad, even though they knew that the man behind them would have to do the same.

'Paulo!' yelled Amber, from behind him. 'We're gonna have to stop!'

'We cannot stop!' yelled Paulo, looking over his shoulder.

For reply, Amber pointed to the black smoke that was still pouring from Alex's machine. Paulo's heart sank and he nodded. Turning back to the trail, he began to look for a place to hide. Up ahead, the trail curved out of sight. Once they were around that bend, they might just have time to split up and hide in the trees before their pursuer arrived. He pointed to the bend and the other four nodded or gave a thumbs-up sign to show that they understood.

By the time the man slewed his machine round the bend, Alpha Force had disappeared from the trail. He brought his snowmobile to a stop and turned off the engine. His breath was loud in the sudden silence, punctuated by the tick of his snowmobile's rapidly cooling engine. Pushing his goggles up on to the top of his head, he pulled the shotgun from its holster and climbed out of the saddle. He took his time as he checked out the deeper snow off-trail. Alpha Force might be hidden from sight, but it was impossible to leave no trace in snow and the tracks of their snowmobiles stood out clearly.

The man frowned. His prey had been clever. They had split up. Five different tracks fanned off from the trail into the trees and he did not know which track would lead him to the camcorder. For a moment he stood indecisively, then his face cleared as he realized it did not matter which track he followed. He picked one at random and began to make his way into the trees.

In her hiding place under the boughs of a fallen spruce, Amber heard the man approaching through the snow. She huddled further under the covering branches and held her breath. She had done her best to cover her tracks. Her footprints marched from her abandoned snowmobile up to the base of the fallen tree, then appeared to step over the trunk and continue onward into the forest. In reality, she had retraced her steps to the trunk, stepping backwards all the way. She had then ducked under the branches and squirmed along to the other end of the fallen tree.

The branches shook above her head as the man stepped up on to the tree trunk and then jumped off again into the snow beyond. Amber's heart was beating so hard, it felt as though it was going to explode out of her chest. The blood sang in her ears and she closed her eyes, hoping against hope that when her footprints ran out, he would not double back. She heard him moving on through the forest with the snow squeaking under his boots. The squeaking grew fainter and fainter, stopped altogether, then started to get louder again. He was heading back to the tree.

Amber groaned, then forced herself to lie still. The branches shook again as the man climbed on to the trunk. The shaking increased as he walked along the top of the trunk towards her, stepping over branches and stopping every few steps to peer at the ground on either side. Amber bit her lip and debated breaking cover and running, but the thought of that sawn-off shotgun kept her pinned to the ground.

The man reached the thinnest part of the trunk and stopped directly above Amber's head. The branches on the other side rustled as he moved them. Amber lay helplessly, waiting for him to do the same on her side. She knew she was going to be caught, but it was still a huge shock when the man plunged his hand through the branches and grabbed her by the back of her hood.

One powerful wrench and she was dragged out of her hiding place. The man let go of her hood, but before she could run, he wrapped his arm around her throat instead. She tried to kick him, but he tightened the crook of his elbow and she started to choke. The man pressed the barrels of the shotgun against the side of her head and she grew still.

'Now we walk back to the trail,' he ordered. 'Slow and steady. We don't want this thing to go off, do we?'

Back at his snowmobile, the man tightened his grip around Amber's throat and brought her to a halt. She lifted her mittened hands and tried to loosen his arm but it was like trying to move a metal bar.

'Hey! Kid with the camcorder!' he called. 'I have your friend here!' He pressed the shotgun harder into the side of Amber's head. 'What's your name?' he asked.

'Amber.' She choked as red spots danced in front of her eyes.

'Amber here is going to die on the count of ten unless you bring me that camcorder. Understand?'

There was silence from the forest. The man started counting.

'One, two . . .'

Hex stood with his back pressed against the trunk of a spruce tree. It was an impossible situation. If he did not give the man the camcorder, Amber would die. If he gave the man the camcorder, Amber would still die, then he would die too.

'. . . five, six . . .' called the man.

Hex closed his eyes. He could wait it out. Call the man's bluff. The more people the man killed, the messier this situation would become – and there was no way to make a shotgun killing look like an accident.

'. . . eight, nine . . .'

With a groan, Hex stepped out from behind the tree. He could not stand back and let Amber die. 'OK, OK,' he called, high-stepping through the deep snow, back to the trail. He was pleased to see that the man's cheek was already swollen and discoloured.

Once he was out on the trail, Hex lifted the camcorder and started filming again. 'So,' he said. 'You planning to kill us all with that shotgun? How're you going to pass that off as an accident? Moose with lethal weapons? I don't think so.'

'How old are you kids?' countered the man. 'Sixteen? Seventeen? Too young to be running around in these parts on your own. They won't find you before the spring thaw. By then, there won't be much left of you. We have some real hungry animals out here, especially through the winter. You will become just another tragic accident. Five unsupervised kids freezing to death.'

'That's good,' said Hex, still filming. 'Keep talking.'

The man's face darkened with anger. He opened his mouth, then stopped and glanced warily from side to side, searching for the Anglo-Chinese girl with a kick like a mule. He was not going to fall for the same trick twice. 'The rest of you!' he called. 'Out here now!'

One by one, Alex, Li and Paulo came out of the trees on to the trail and stood shoulder to shoulder with Hex.

'Kneel down,' ordered the man. 'Hands behind your heads.'

They all obeyed, except Hex, who kneeled but continued to film. The man marched Amber forward until she was standing in front of Hex. 'Give her the camcorder,' he said.

Hex looked up at Amber and she looked down as best she could with the man's arm locked round her throat and a shotgun digging into the side of her head. She stretched out her hands for the camcorder but Hex held back. Once this man had the evidence, it was all over for them. His mind raced, trying to find a solution. There must be something he could do!

Amber began to choke as the man tightened his grip and Hex's mind went blank. Reluctantly, he handed over the camcorder. The man dragged Amber back along the trail and then forced her to her knees. As the shotgun barrels moved round to the back of her neck, Amber looked hopelessly at the others. Her eyes were full of fear and big with unshed tears.

Alex tensed. The only chance now was for the four of them to rush the man. He would start firing immediately, but some of them might survive long enough to overwhelm him. If not, then at least they would die fighting, which had to be better than kneeling in the snow and waiting to be slaughtered. He glanced at Li, Hex and Paulo and saw the same determination in their eyes.

'On the count of three,' whispered Alex. 'One, two—'

He stopped counting as a roar echoed along the trail. An instant later, a huge, white shape burst out of the trees and reared up on its hind legs behind the man.

'It is Cyclops!' cried Paulo as the great bear roared again.

After one horrified glance behind him, the man kicked Amber out of his way and ran for his snowmobile, leaving her sprawled at the bear's feet.

Seven

Any other bear would have gone for the easier target, but this bear only had one eye and Amber was lying on its blind side. Cyclops ignored her. Instead, it went down on all fours, slamming its left paw into the snow centimetres away from her head, and took off after the man.

With a scream of terror, the man flung himself over to the other side of his snowmobile as Cyclops reared up and swiped at him with a huge paw. The bear came down on the little machine with such force, the fuel tank collapsed in on itself, spraying petrol everywhere.

With a snarl, the bear knocked the snowmobile out of its way to get to the man cowering in the snow. Again, it swiped at the man and this time its paw made contact with his head. The force of the blow snapped his neck and sent a spray of blood, bone and brains flying through the air. The man's body rolled and came to a stop very close to Amber, who was still sprawled on the ground clutching the camcorder. Hex surged to his feet and grabbed her under the arms, dragging her out of the way as the bear reared up again and roared a challenge.

'Everybody down and stay still!' cried Li. 'And don't look it in the eye. Bears see that as a threat.'

They crouched in the snow, keeping their eyes down. The bear glared at them all for a moment longer, then went down on to all fours and turned back to the body. With one rip of its claws, it opened up the man from neck to groin. Cottony flakes of jacket insulation floated up into the air, then down again to land in the spreading pool of blood around the body. The dead man's eyes stared sightlessly at the sky as the bear dipped its snout and began to eat.

Paulo thought he was going to be sick. He turned

his head away and managed to swallow down the bile that rose in his throat. 'We must go while the bear is occupied,' he whispered to the others.

'What about him?' asked Alex, pointing to the body.

Paulo looked, then quickly looked away again. 'We can do nothing for him now. We must get away before the bear loses interest in him and turns on us.'

Alex nodded. They started to clamber to their feet, but the bear reared up and towered over them with a full-throated roar. It made a fearsome sight, standing three metres tall, gouts of blood dripping from its jaws. Quickly, Alpha Force sank to the ground again and the bear returned to its meal, watching them closely with its one eye. They were trapped. Their snowmobiles were scattered and too far away to make a run for it, and there was always the possibility that Alex's machine would not start again.

'What now?' asked Hex, looking at Li, their animal behaviour expert.

Li wiped the sweat from her forehead and thought for a few seconds, then her eyes brightened as she had an idea. 'Can we get hold of the guy's shotgun?'

For answer, Amber pointed out the handle of the shotgun, poking out from under the man's body.

'Oh,' said Li.

'But we have the – how do you say? – the tranquillizer rifle,' said Paulo. His English was now extremely good after his years with Alpha Force, but he still had trouble with the occasional word, particularly in times of stress.

Hex shook his head. 'It's back there in the snowmobile trailer.'

They all looked at Li again. 'Um,' she said, thinking desperately. 'If we could really scare it somehow . . .'

'How?' hissed Amber.

Li shrugged. She was all out of ideas.

'Would an explosion do it?' asked Alex, staring thoughtfully at the man's overturned snowmobile.

'Of course,' said Li. 'All animals are afraid of fire.'

Alex unzipped the pouch attached to his belt and pulled out his survival tin. His dad was in the SAS and always carried a survival tin as part of his basic kit. He had shown Alex how to put his own tin together and Alex now carried this small, battered metal container with him everywhere. It had saved his life and the lives of the other members of Alpha Force on a number of occasions, and he was hoping it would do so again now. Although it was only the size of a large tobacco tin, it was tightly packed with essential items. Inside there were needles and thread, fish-hooks and a line, a tiny medical kit, a flint, a magnifying glass, a compass and beta light, snare wire, a flexible saw, a tightly folded survival bag made of heat-insulated reflective material, a ball of dry kindling, a candle and a strip of matches.

It was the matches Alex reached for now, before replacing the lid on the tin and slipping it back into his pouch. Carefully he removed his outer mittens, then he tore the first match from the strip and ran the head across the striker. The match was good and dry and flared immediately. Quickly, Alex cupped it with his other hand until the flame was strong, then he flicked the match towards the fuel-soaked snow around the damaged snowmobile. The match fell well short. The flame fluttered and went out. With a soft curse, Alex tore off another match and tried again. The match landed nearer to the snowmobile but, once again, the snow snuffed out the flame.

'C'mon!' hissed Amber, staring fearfully at the bear a few metres away.

Alex frowned, thinking hard. Then his face cleared as an idea came to him. He stripped the thin, inner glove from his left hand, then plunged his hand down through the snow until he reached the frozen ground of the trail. His fingers began to ache, then hurt, and then grow numb as he scrabbled around under the snow. Finally, he found what he was looking for. He pulled his hand out of the snow with a small stone clutched in his blue fingers.

Alex blew on his hand to warm it, then pulled his inner glove on again. Opening the survival tin for a second time, he removed a small amount of the kindling material and wrapped it around the stone. Finally, he struck a third match and held it to the kindling until it was burning so well, he was in danger of setting fire to his glove.

'Here goes,' whispered Alex.

He took aim and threw the stone. It landed right in the middle of the fuel-soaked area around the snow-mobile. For a second, nothing happened. Then the ground burst into flames with an explosive whump.

Cyclops flinched away from the flames, then, instead of running, he turned back and reared up on to his hind legs with a roar.

'It's not working!' hissed Amber, but Alex was watching a twisting snake of flame wriggle towards the snowmobile's fuel tank. An instant later, a second, much bigger explosion sent bellowing gouts of flame up as high as the tree tops. Alpha Force flattened themselves into the snow as a blast of scorching air spread outwards from the centre of the explosion.

Cyclops roared again, but this time it was more of a scream. Alpha Force raised their heads, shielding their faces against the heat of the flames. The bear was down on all fours, swatting at its scorched nose. All down one side, its fur was blackened and smoking. The bear flinched sideways as a second explosion came from the burning snowmobile, then the huge beast turned tail and ran. Alpha Force sat up and listened to the bear crashing away through the forest as fast as it could go.

'Missing you already,' muttered Hex, staggering to his feet. He hurried over to the dead man and began going through the pockets of the tattered jacket, trying not to look too closely at what the bear had done to the body.

Amber looked around with a dazed expression, as though she could not quite believe she was still alive. She began to shake and the shaking grew stronger and stronger, until her teeth were chattering uncontrollably. Li shuffled over and put her arms around her friend.

'Amber?' said Alex. 'Are you ready to move out?'

'Give her a minute, can't you?' demanded Li.

'We don't have a minute,' said Alex quietly.

'But the bear – it will not return,' said Paulo.

'It's not the bear I'm worried about.' Alex nodded over at the body. 'There might be more like him.'

Amber, Li and Paulo looked up at him in shocked understanding. There could be more than one killer out there. The man could have a partner, or even a whole team working for him.

'OK. I'm OK,' said Amber, climbing to her feet and bracing her knees to stop her legs from shaking.

'Where do we go?' asked Paulo, as Hex returned to the group, stuffing something into an inside pocket of his jacket.

'Away from here,' said Alex, glancing up at the column of thick, black smoke rising above the tree tops. 'If there are more killers in the area, this smoke is going to bring them running. We'll head inland. Hudson Bay is not a good place to be right now.'

After an hour of travelling, Alex began to look out for a good, sheltered stopping place. The smoke from the burning snowmobile was far enough behind them now and he was worried about the way his own machine was performing. It had taken several tries to start it and the engine note was rough and uneven. The wind had dropped as they made their way inland through the darkening day, but so had the temperature. According to the digital thermometer display on his dashboard, it was now twenty-five below zero, and even with their layers of arctic gear they were all beginning to feel the cold. At first Alex had been sweating behind his goggles, but now the sweat that had collected in his eyebrows had formed a crackling layer of frost and his nostrils were becoming blocked with plugs of ice.

He spotted a particularly thick stand of spruce

trees and motioned the others to a halt. They waited with their engines idling while he studied the spot. The outer trees on one side of the stand were flagged. This meant that the branches only grew on one side of the trunk, giving the tree the appearance of a flag on a pole. The flagged trees were a good indication of the direction of the prevailing wind and this was important in choosing a good spot to camp. It would not be a good idea to set up a shelter on a calm evening, only to find a howling gale blowing through the entrance the next morning.

Alex pointed to the lee side of the stand of trees and they set off again, driving slowly along until he spotted what he wanted. Three spruce trees were growing shoulder to shoulder in a line, so close together that their lower branches merged together under their covering of snow. He brought his spluttering snowmobile to a halt in front of the three spruce trees and turned off the engine. The others parked up beside him one by one and turned off their engines too. The deep silence of the interior settled around them as they eased off their goggles and clambered stiffly from their machines.

'Fingers? Toes?' asked Alex. His face was so stiff with cold, the words came out slurred, but the others knew what he meant. They each checked for any sign of pins and needles or numbness that could be the start of frostbite. Next, Alex peered into each face in turn, checking noses and cheekbones. They all looked fine, just pinched with cold and tiredness.

Amber raised her frosted eyebrows, which looked very white next to her dark skin. 'Do we pass inspection?' she asked.

Alex grinned, pleased to see that she was back to her old, sarcastic self. 'Yes. You pass. And here's your reward.'

He reached inside his outer jacket and removed a small cloth bag which was hanging from his neck by a cord. He opened the drawstring and produced five bars of chocolate.

'Oh! I love you!' yelled Amber, tearing off her outer gloves and grabbing one of the chocolate bars. She ripped off the packaging and crammed the chocolate into her mouth. ''Sgood,' she mumbled.

Everyone else grabbed a bar and began to eat as though they had not seen food for days. In such low temperatures their bodies used up huge amounts of energy just to stay warm, and since they had arrived in northern Canada they had all discovered a craving for fat in any shape or form. Here, even Amber could safely eat chocolate without worrying about blood sugar levels because she would burn it all up again within a couple of hours.

'Now, that is what I call survival expertise,' said Paulo, grinning at Alex with chocolate-coated teeth. Paulo knew that all the food in the trailers would be frozen solid and he had not been looking forward to the long, drawn-out process of lighting a fire and thawing everything out before they could start cooking. 'It is a good trick,' he added. 'Wearing your food. I shall have to remember that.'

Paulo looked down at Li, expecting her to meet his gaze with laughter sparkling in her uptilted eyes. Instead, she stood next to him, silent and pale, gazing back the way they had come. There was an awkward silence as the rest of Alpha Force remembered that Li had lost a dear friend that day.

'Right,' said Alex, breaking the silence. 'We've had our energy boost. Now let's make camp.'

Eight

Alex had chosen the three spruce trees because of their spreading, interlinking lower branches. Snow had built up on the top side of the branches, weighing them down so that they bent to the ground. More snow had piled up around the outside of the bent branches, effectively anchoring them in place. Underneath the tent-like branches, where the snow could no longer reach, a natural hollow had formed.

Once they had unloaded the snow shovels from the trailers, Alex showed Amber and Hex how to dig down carefully into the snow beneath the trees to enlarge the existing hollow without disturbing the outer branches. Li and Paulo set off into the trees to collect as much dead wood as they could find. They were going to need huge amounts of fuel to keep them warm through a night of sub-zero temperatures. Alex concentrated on getting a fire going. First, he dug out a fire pit in front of their shelter trees. Using the snow he had dug out and the snow that Amber and Hex were clearing from under the trees, he built a snow bank behind the fire pit to create extra shelter and reflect the heat from the fire back into the hollows under the trees.

Starting with a pyramid of small, dry twigs and another piece of his precious kindling, Alex used his flint to create a spark. Soon the kindling and twigs were burning well and he began building up the fire by adding branches from Li and Paulo's first load of dead wood. Once he had a good blaze going, he filled two billycans with snow and set them on the edges of the fire to melt, then he strapped on his snowshoes and set off towards a willow thicket he had noted on the way in. Rabbits and snowshoe hares were common in this region and they loved to eat willow bark. Alpha Force were carrying a limited supply of food but Alex wanted to supplement it in case they had to stay hidden for a while.

The sun was starting to set as he tramped through the snow towards the willow thicket and everything had an edging of gold. Alex smiled as he looked around. He felt at home in northern Canada. It reminded him of some of the remoter forests and moors back home in Northumberland. His sharp eyes noted a group of ptarmigan under a spruce tree. The birds were pure white and almost perfectly camouflaged against the snow, but they were scratching for food under the trees and the movement of their large, densely feathered feet had caught his eye.

Alex stopped, debating whether to try to catch one, but then he saw that another hunter was already stalking the birds. An arctic fox was stepping slowly through the snow, weaving along the edge of the tree line. The fox already had its white winter coat, which was perfectly adapted for cold-climate survival. Each hair of the coat was hollow inside and full of air. This worked like the layer of air in a double-glazing unit, trapping the fox's body warmth and enabling it to tolerate temperatures as low as forty below zero.

As Alex watched, the fox reached the tree next to the ptarmigan and flattened itself into the snow, preparing to pounce. An instant later, it launched itself at the birds. They rose up into the air and flew off in a flurry of feathers and squawks.

Alex thought they had all managed to escape, but when he looked again at the fox, it was trotting off with a bird hanging limply from its jaws. He smiled in admiration for a hunter that could catch its prey without the use of snares or traps. He also made a note to check his snares before morning. If he did not retrieve his catch pretty quickly, the fox would eat it right out of the snare.

When he reached the thicket, Alex was pleased to see that there were several trails through the snow made by rabbits or hares. Pulling off his outer mittens, he took the snare wire from his survival tin and set to work. He fashioned a slipknot noose out of the brass snare wire and then rubbed the metal with rabbit droppings to dull the shine and hide any human smell. Next, he hung the snare from a willow branch overhanging one of the trails. Finally, he blocked the sides of the trail with a fence of small sticks. This would funnel the rabbit into middle of the trail and it would run straight into his snare. The noose would instantly tighten around the rabbit's neck, cutting off its air supply and killing it quickly.

Alex set a dozen traps in the willow thicket, reckoning that he would catch three or four rabbits if he was lucky. By the time he got back to the camp site, Amber and Hex had finished the shelters. Each hollow had a sleeping platform made of snow, which Amber and Hex had tramped down with their snowshoes and then covered with spruce boughs to create an insulating mattress for their sleeping bags. Paulo and Li had collected a huge pile of dead wood, including two sections of tree trunk which they had set in front of the fire to serve as seats. Paulo had made a hot drink for everyone by adding stock cubes to the first batch of melted snow and now two more billycans were strung over the fire, heating up five boil-in-the-bag meals. Paulo had also placed a large, flat stone on the edge of the fire where he was slow-baking flat, savoury biscuits made from oatmeal and melted snow. A large pat of butter was thawing next to the stone, ready to spread on the biscuits when they were done.

Alex sat down and accepted his share of the stock-cube drink. For a moment, everything was quiet as Alpha Force sat staring into the fire, lost in their private thoughts. Then Alex straightened and looked around the circle.

'Time to talk,' he said. 'Who wants to start?'

'Me,' said Hex, and everyone looked at him in surprise. Usually, when they had a problem to solve, Hex preferred to sit back and listen to them flounder for a while, before coming in with a devastatingly neat and logical solution.

Hex smiled wryly at their surprised expressions, then he reached into the inner pocket of his jacket and pulled out the object he had taken from their pursuer's body. It was a mobile phone.

'His?' asked Amber, jerking her thumb back the way they had come.

'Yes. This is what gave him away, remember?'

They nodded, remembering how the man's phone had started ringing as they stood in a shocked circle around Papaluk's frozen body. 'I took it because I wanted to know who was calling him,' continued Hex. He stripped off his gloves, switched on the phone and studied the display. 'Text message,' he muttered, accessing the menu.

They were silent, listening to the beeps as Hex negotiated his way around the phone, stopping every now and then to read the information on the display. 'OK,' he said finally. 'Here's what we have. Just after he killed Papaluk, he sent a text message to some guy called "D". The message he sent reads, "Original leak sealed. Poss. 5 more. Total containment?"'

Hex lifted his eyes from the screen and watched the others absorb the meaning of the text message.

'I am thinking our own Papaluk was the original leak,' said Paulo, sending Li a sympathetic glance.

'And by "sealed" he means he killed her!' growled Amber.

'And we must be the five more possible leaks,' said Paulo.

'So, when he talks about total containment, he's asking D whether he should kill us too,' said Alex flatly.

'What was D's reply?' asked Amber.

For answer, Hex pressed a button and turned the phone so that they could all see the one word on the screen. 'Yes.'

'That's why the guy was hiding to start with,' said Hex. 'He was waiting for instructions from his boss.'

'And his boss told him to kill us,' said Alex.

'Just who the hell is this D guy?' demanded Amber.

'Let's find out,' said Hex. He checked the last number dialled and hit the redial button. The phone connected and they all gathered round to hear who picked up at the other end. They got a recorded voice.

'Daniel Usher is busy. Leave a message.'

'So, D stands for Daniel Usher, the head of Usher Mining Corporation,' drawled Hex, breaking the connection.

'He is not polite,' commented Paulo.

Hex smiled without humour. '"Not polite". That's one way of describing him. "Murderer" is another.'

'I – you know, guys, I—' Amber came to a halt with a look of intense concentration on her face. 'I think I know that voice – I just can't place it . . .'

Hex reached inside his jacket and brought out the soft leather pouch that held his palm-sized PC. Quickly, he slipped the little computer from the bag and lifted the lid. The palmtop had been a gift from Amber. It had come straight from the development labs and was so technologically advanced it was not yet available on the open market. There was a flat aerial in the lid which could give access to the Net via the nearest communications satellite. Within minutes, Hex was connected. His fingers danced across the little keyboard as he began his search for information on Daniel Usher. He started with the official Usher Mining Corporation site. As he had hoped, there was a glossy colour image of Daniel Usher smiling out of the screen. He was a white man in his early forties, tanned and fit looking, with blue eyes and thick, dark hair, greying at the temples. His smile was warm and wide and his eyes stared confidently from the screen.

'Does that help?' he asked, turning the screen so that Amber could see it.

Amber gasped. 'That slimeball!' she cried. 'Sure I remember him! He's one of the richest guys in

America. He has his fingers in all sorts of pies. He used to show up at some of my parents' parties, before they sold the business and got out of that whole scene.'

'He was a family friend?' asked Paulo.

'Nah! My parents thought he was a slimeball too.'

'Why did they ask him to their parties, if they didn't like him?' asked Alex.

'They weren't the sort of parties you asked your friends to,' said Amber with a sigh, remembering the long, boring hours spent in her parents' New York penthouse, talking to people she didn't know and smiling at people she didn't like.

'What other sort of parties are there?' asked Alex, his face a picture of puzzlement in the firelight.

'Aw, hell, you know. Schmoozing, politics, wheeler-dealing . . .' Amber faltered to a halt, at a loss as to how to explain the sort of corporate entertainment her parents had dutifully provided before they decided to turn their backs on all that. Parties where someone else wrote the guest list, prepared the food and served the drinks.

'You know. Business parties . . .' finished Amber

lamely. She and Alex stared at one another across the fire. They were less than a metre apart but there was suddenly a wide gulf between the rich American girl and the boy from a village in Northumberland.

The silence stretched out until finally Alex shook his head.

'What!' demanded Amber.

'Rich people,' said Alex. 'All that money and they still can't throw a good knees-up.'

He grinned and Amber grinned back. 'Yeah, but I can throw a good snowball,' she said, grabbing a double handful of snow and preparing to lob it at Alex. He pounced on her, knocking the snowball from her hands. Amber fell off the back of the log and, as Alex reached out a hand to help her up, she pulled him down into the snow after her.

Paulo laughed and turned to Li, expecting her to be up on her feet and ready to join in. Li did not even raise her head and Paulo's smile disappeared like a light going out. Amber and Alex shared a look, then got to their feet and brushed the snow from their clothes.

'When you two have finished rolling about,'

drawled Hex, without looking up from the screen of his palmtop, 'you might want to hear what I've found out so far. On the surface, Daniel Usher is squeaky-clean. Your basic all-American guy. As well as Usher Mining, he owns a chain of retail stores and one of the biggest television companies in the US. He's even planning to run for governor in his home state. He'll be launching his electoral campaign in a few days' time with a live broadcast on his own television channel. Of course, he's keen to stress that he's paying for the airtime just like any other murderer— I mean, just like any other candidate.'

'Yeah, right,' sneered Amber. 'OK. So that's the public face. Now, go on. Do what you do best, Hex.'

Hex interlaced his fingers and flexed them so that the knuckle joints popped. Then, hunching over the little keyboard, he began to explore behind the public face of Daniel Usher. First he entered a university computer system and used a password to get into an obscure corner where he had stored his lock-picking tools. These were programs he had written which would gain him access to sites on the

Net that were forbidden to most users. His lock-picking programs were not strictly legal and so, like most hackers, Hex stored them on a large, multi-user system rather than on his own personal hard drive.

Once he had downloaded the programs, he got to work uncovering Daniel Usher's less public connections. He worked with intense concentration, ignoring the others as they moved around him, serving up the food or tending to the fire. Finally, he sat back with a satisfied smile. 'Oh, yes. I've got him. He's involved in a number of really sleazy money-making schemes around the world, but he keeps his name well out of it.'

'What sort of schemes?' asked Paulo, handing Hex a plate of stew and a thickly buttered oatmeal biscuit.

'Sweatshops in Korea,' mumbled Hex around a mouthful of stew. 'Making clothes. Three women who tried to fight for better working conditions there were found drowned in a river. Sound familiar?'

Alex nodded grimly. 'What else?' he asked.

'There's a chemical factory in Mexico merrily

sending all sorts of crud out into the environment but the locals are so scared, they daren't make a fuss. There's a dam-building project in India with rumours of bribery and corruption. There's a—'

'Hang on,' said Amber, sitting up sharply. 'Just re-wind a bit. The company building that dam. Does it have a name?'

Hex looked at his screen. 'Goliath something . . .'

'Enterprise,' finished Amber quietly. 'Goliath Enterprise.'

'How did you know that?' asked Hex.

'My mom and dad were trying to get that project stopped when they were killed. A whole bunch of local protestors died in a coach accident on the same day. We think they had managed to find evidence to prove the corruption rumours that were hanging around the project like a bad smell and they were about to go public when they were all killed. The police investigated Goliath Enterprise, but the so-called company directors were only front men. When the police tried to find the real power behind the company, they just kept coming up against a blank wall.'

Amber swallowed hard and looked around the firelit circle, then back to Hex. 'You know what, Hex?' she said, in a soft, trembling voice. 'I think you just found the guy who killed my parents.'

There was a moment of stunned silence. Hex watched Amber as the tears filled her eyes and spilled over on to her cheeks. His own eyes grew hard and determined, like chips of green ice. 'Right,' he said, picking up his palmtop. 'Let's get him.'

'How do we do that?' asked Paulo.

'We have the evidence,' said Hex, opening up his e-mail facility. 'The underwater camcorder's digital. It has firewire technology, which means I can download the images into my palmtop right now. Then I can send them to anyone, anywhere in the world.' Hex looked up at the others with his fingers poised over the keys. 'All we have to decide is who to e-mail first.'

'The local police,' said Alex. 'They can get out to the mine the fastest.'

'Or Papaluk's employers,' said Paulo. 'They are a multi-national agency. They will know what to do.'

'No-one,' said Amber. 'We tell no-one.' She looked at Li and the two girls shared a glance of total understanding. Amber nodded to Li, who turned to face the three boys. She had hardly spoken since the discovery of Papaluk's body, but her voice was hard and icy clear now.

'This is personal,' she said. 'We go in on our own.'

NINE

'We go in on our own?' repeated Paulo, in astonishment.

'Is there an echo round here?' said Amber, raising her eyebrows at Li.

Alex frowned. 'Listen, I understand how much you two want to get your revenge, but revenge is a bad basis for any operation.'

'It seems a pretty good basis to me,' said Li, staring at Alex with a cold fire in her eyes.

'What I mean is, if you're running on emotions, then you're not using your head. That's when things go wrong.'

'Look, it's not only revenge,' said Li, relenting a little. 'The thing is, once we tell the authorities, everything slows down. Any investigation has to be done officially. And by the time they manage to wade through all the paperwork and legal stuff to get access to the mine, you can be sure there will be absolutely no evidence of cyanide dumping or anything else. But if we go in quick, quiet and secret, then Usher Mining Corporation won't have time to clean up their act first.'

'C'mon, guys,' said Amber. 'This is why Alpha Force was set up! To do the stuff the authorities aren't allowed to do.'

'But we already have evidence!' cried Hex. 'The camcorder footage—'

'—does nothing to incriminate Daniel Usher,' interrupted Li. 'He'll say something like, "Oh, that's just a guy who happened to work at the mine. He loved Papaluk, went crazy when she rejected him. Nothing to do with me . . ."'

Hex nodded reluctantly. 'And the text messages are too vague. They could have any number of meanings. You're right. We need more.'

'You're forgetting one thing,' said Alex. 'Daniel Usher's hired killer is lying under a spruce tree in several pieces. What happens when he doesn't report in?'

Hex pulled the man's mobile phone from his pocket and stared at it thoughtfully. 'Perhaps he should send his boss a text message. Something like, "Tracking leaks. May take a few days to arrange containment." That should buy us some time.'

He looked around at the others, raising his eyebrows questioningly. Li and Amber nodded immediately. Paulo looked at Li's brightening face and nodded too. Alex hesitated, then bowed to the majority verdict. 'OK,' he said. 'We go in on our own.'

They each spent the rest of the evening preparing in their own way for the mission ahead. Hex stayed by the blazing fire, hunched over his palmtop. He was searching the Net to find out as much as he could about the layout of the mine.

Amber strapped on her snowshoes, gathered a bundle of thin, straight branches from the woodpile, and walked out into the darkness. Standing with her back to the fire, she waited until her night vision was sharp and strong. She had to work out their route, and for that she needed to see the stars. She reckoned that the mine was roughly thirty miles west of their present position. The simplest way to find the mine would be to travel inland along the frozen river where the cyanide had been dumped. The river would lead them to the mine, but first she had to find the river. She knew it was to the south, and unless they had veered further north than she thought on their escape inland, it should not be too far away. Amber was betting that if they headed south the next morning they would come across the river within an hour.

Amber had a compass, but she did not entirely trust it. Compasses could be unreliable this close to the North Pole, but the stars never changed. The night sky was clear and full of stars. Quickly, she picked out two constellations, the Plough and Cassiopeia. Once she had these, she could find the Pole Star by imagining a straight line between them. The Pole Star was in the middle of that line and it shone directly above the North Pole.

'Gotcha,' muttered Amber, gazing up at the Pole Star. Now it was a simple matter to figure out their direction for the morning. Amber took her bundle of sticks and stuck them into the snow in a straight line, with an arrowhead at the end pointing the way south.

Paulo, Li and Alex worked on the snowmobiles. Li and Alex took care of the simpler stuff, checking oil and topping up fuel on the other four snowmobiles, while Paulo checked out Alex's machine. It had been sounding rougher and rougher on the journey inland and Paulo suspected that there was a major problem. His suspicions were confirmed when the engine would not start.

'*Dios*,' he muttered, lifting the cowling to look at the engine. He stripped off his outer mittens but kept the thin under-gloves on. The night-time temperature was touching thirty below zero and he did not want to leave his fingertips stuck to the engine. Paulo always carried a basic toolkit in his belt pouch. He opened it now and began working his way methodically around the engine by the light of his torch. Finally, he slammed the cowling back into place with a curse, packed away his tools and stamped back to the warmth of the fire.

'That doesn't sound good,' said Amber, coming to join the others.

Paulo sighed, holding his hands out to the fire to warm them before replacing his mittens. 'It is not good. It is shooted.'

'Shot,' laughed Amber, unstrapping her snow-shoes. 'You mean it's shot.'

'What's wrong with it?' asked Alex.

'It is the fuel pump,' said Paulo. 'The fuel pump is shotted. It is burned out, Alex, and we do not have a replacement.'

'Yeah, but we can still complete the mission,' said Li hastily. 'These snowmobiles will carry two people. Alex can share with someone.'

'Me,' said Amber. 'He can ride with me. You can even drive if you want, Alex,' she added generously.

'Gee, thanks,' said Alex, raising his eyebrows at her. Everyone knew that Amber hated machines. She was much happier with forms of transport that did not require engines, such as her yacht or her thoroughbred horses. Amber grinned at Alex without a hint of embarrassment.

'Will it carry two people on the sort of journey we're planning?' asked Alex, looking at Paulo.

'Of course it will,' said Li. 'Won't it, Paulo?'

'I think we must lose the trailer,' said Paulo.

'But that's two trailer-loads of stuff!' said Amber. 'Alex's and mine. Can we afford to leave so much behind?'

'We can redistribute,' said Li. 'We can get rid of the tents for a start. We didn't need them tonight, did we? And we could leave the diving gear—'

'I think we should hang on to the dry suits,' interrupted Hex, looking up from his screen. 'I've been checking out the layout of the mine. They're very security conscious. The front way in is patrolled and floodlit, so we may have to go in the back way.'

'Which is?' asked Amber.

'Into the old, abandoned mine workings, from the river.'

'OK, then,' said Li. 'But we'd only need a couple of dry suits. Two in, the rest on land, right? It's diving protocol. We can dump the other suits and that'll leave plenty of room for the essentials, won't it, Alex?'

Everyone looked at Alex. Would three trailers carry all they needed to survive in the interior? As their survival expert, the final decision had to be his. Alex hesitated. Three trailer-loads would be cutting it fine. He looked around at the others, weighing up all the variables. He was the only one in the group with experience of cold-climate survival. On the other hand, if he had to choose anyone as travelling companions, it would be the other four members of Alpha Force. He would trust them with his life. It was as simple as that. Alex looked over at Li, who was watching him intently, waiting for his decision.

'All right,' said Alex, standing up. 'Let's reload.'

An hour later, it was done. A neat stockpile of tents, spare diving equipment and supplies was hidden in the trees alongside the crippled snowmobile and the two spare trailers. The three remaining trailers were packed and ready to go.

'I'll take first watch,' said Alex as they all headed for their sleeping bags. 'Two hours. Then, Hex, you take second watch.'

Hex groaned. 'Are you sure we need to set a watch?' he yawned. 'The more I think about it, the more I'm sure that guy was operating alone.'

'Besides,' added Amber. 'If someone else was following us, they'd've been here by now.'

Alex shook his head. What Hex and Amber said made perfect sense, but he could see the tracks of their snowmobiles cutting across the snowfield in front of the trees. The tracks stood out clearly in the moonlight, pointing the way straight to the camp.

'I'd just feel more comfortable if we set a watch,' he said. 'Even if there's no-one out there looking for us, there are still the bears to think about. They can smell food from twenty miles away – and we've been cooking.'

The others headed for bed and Alex piled fresh wood on to the fire. He laughed softly as he listened to Hex grumble his way into his sleeping bag. Gradually, the muffled curses and mutterings about unnecessary watches subsided into silence and Alex was left alone by the fire. He did not mind. He was solitary by nature and he was never happier than when he was outdoors.

He sat for an hour, feeding the fire and letting the peace of the night settle over him, then he strapped on his snowshoes and went to check the willow thicket. He was pleased to find two rabbits and a hare in the snares. Now that Alpha Force had jettisoned some of their supplies, it was even more important to find what food they could on the way. Alex laid his catch out on the snow, then dismantled all his snares. They were leaving early in the morning and a responsible trapper never left snares in place when he would not be around to check them regularly. The snares had killed the rabbits swiftly and humanely, but a larger animal could catch a foot in the wire and slowly starve to death.

Taking his single-bladed survival knife from its sheath at his belt, he got to work skinning and gutting the catch. He left the innards and heads in a pile on the edge of the thicket as a gift for the arctic fox, then he headed back to camp.

Back at the fire, Alex packed his catch into the foil containers that had held the boil-in-the-bag meals, then he buried the three parcels in the hot wood ash on the edge of the fire. The meat would slow-bake in the ashes and provide them with a tasty, hot breakfast in the morning. Finally, he sat down on the tree-trunk seat and cleaned and sharpened his knife. Once he was satisfied, he slipped the knife back into its sheath and checked the time. His two-hour watch was over. It was time to wake Hex.

Alex turned towards the tree shelters and saw that Li was sitting up in her sleeping bag, gazing out at him. He ducked under the branches and sat beside her on the snow platform. Amber was snoring softly behind them, completely hidden inside her thick, down sleeping bag.

'Thanks,' said Li softly.

'What for?' asked Alex.

'For deciding the mission could carry on,' said Li.

Alex nodded and they were silent for a while.

'She was like a big sister to me,' whispered Li, gazing out at the fire. Alex reached out and squeezed Li's thin shoulder. Her lip quivered but she remained dry-eyed.

'Don't disturb Hex,' she whispered. 'I'll do the next watch. I can't sleep anyway.'

Alex climbed into his sleeping bag. A clean,

pine-needle smell rose up around him as he settled back on to the cushioned springiness of the spruce boughs. The bag wrapped him in warmth from head to foot, and soon his eyelids began to droop. The last thing he saw before he fell into an exhausted sleep was Li's silhouetted profile as she sat beside the fire, thinking about the big sister she had lost that day.

Ten

'Are you sure it'll hold us?' asked Amber fearfully, gripping Alex by the shoulders as he prepared to ease the snowmobile down the river bank and on to the snow-covered ice. It was the morning of the next day and, after leaving their camp before dawn, Alpha Force had successfully completed the first part of their journey. They had reached the river that would lead them to the mine.

Alex sighed. 'Amber, I've been down and checked it. I even used the ice drill. That ice is at least a metre thick.'

'Yeah, but the ice in Hudson Bay was really thin—'

'Forget Hudson Bay! That was seawater. The salt in seawater means it has a much lower freezing point than freshwater. And what sort of water do we have in the river?'

'Freshwater,' muttered Amber.

'Plus,' continued Alex, 'temperatures are much lower here than they were on the coast.'

'What's the hold-up?' called Li, behind them. She was standing up on her snowmobile, anxious to move on.

'Nothing!' called Alex. 'Listen,' he said to Amber in a lower voice. 'That river surface has been frozen solid for weeks now. OK?'

'OK,' said Amber, but her fingers dug into Alex's shoulders hard enough to make him wince.

'Hey, ease off,' he said.

'Sorry,' muttered Amber, fractionally reducing the pressure.

'You can relax now,' called Alex as he guided the snowmobile down the bank. 'You've done your bit. You led us to the river!'

The snowmobile reached the bottom of the bank

and shot out on to the ice. It was rough going at first as they rattled up and down over the pressure ridges that had formed at the edge of the river as it froze, and Amber did not let go of Alex's shoulders until they reached the smoother ice in the middle.

'OK,' she said cautiously, looking around. Then, more confidently, 'Let's go!'

Alex swung the snowmobile round and opened up the throttle. Li, Paulo and Hex pulled in behind and the four snowmobiles headed upriver towards the mine. At first the sun was bright and the river was wide, which made the travelling easy, but as they moved further inland, the river grew narrower and more twisted. The snow cover grew thicker, sometimes hiding the pressure ridges that corrugated the ice on every curve. The banks steepened until the low sun could not penetrate to river level, and Alpha Force had to turn their headlights full on as they travelled along the dark, cold tunnel between the banks.

They were all well wrapped up and had the drawstrings of their hoods pulled tight around their goggles so that their faces were completely covered, but gradually the chill began to seep into their bones. The wind picked up and a bank of threatening, grey clouds rolled in. Finally, with no sign of the mine, Alex decided it was time to find a place to stop. They all needed a rest and some hot food. He began to scan the banks for a slope that was gentle enough for the snowmobiles to climb.

And that was when disaster struck.

If Alex had been giving his full attention to the terrain ahead of the snowmobiles, he might have spotted the danger signs in his headlight beams. Instead, he kept scanning the banks and driving straight towards a circular patch on the frozen river where the snow cover was seamed with cracks. Wisps of steam were rising through the cracks – a warning that there was open water running beneath the covering of snow. Alex was heading straight for a massive suck hole in the ice: a frozen whirlpool, twisting right through the ice to the flowing river below; the opening at the bottom of this particular suck hole was big enough to swallow a snowmobile.

The front skis of the snowmobile tipped over the lip of the suck hole and Amber screamed in fright as, suddenly, the snow collapsed beneath them. Then everything happened with nightmare speed. The snowmobile upended and slid down the side of the frozen whirlpool with its headlight beams bouncing crazily off the walls of ice. Alex saw the rushing black water at the bottom of the slope and instinctively stuck his feet out, trying to brake in thin air. The snowmobile tipped and Alex yelled in pain as his outstretched leg scraped down the wall of ice. The added friction was enough to make the snowmobile turn sideways and come to a jolting halt, jammed across the narrowest part of the suck hole.

The headlights still lit up the whole scene and Alex could see that they were hanging centimetres above the rushing black water at the bottom of the hole. The front of the snowmobile was balanced on the very tips of its skis and the back of the caterpillar tracks were jammed on a tree branch that was frozen into the wall of the suck hole. Alex looked up. The ice layer was just over two metres thick here, which meant that the surface was only a metre above his head, but it might as well have been a mile away. The suck hole was shaped like a shallow, wide-topped funnel, twisting and turning its way down to the water: there were metres of sloping, slick ice walls to climb to reach safety.

The engine was still whining, making the whole machine shudder and filling the suck hole with exhaust fumes as it tried to turn the jammed caterpillar tracks. As Alex watched in horror, the tracks jumped once, twice, and the branch began to splinter. Quickly, he reached out and turned off the ignition. They were plunged into darkness as the engine cut out and the headlights winked off. For a few seconds more, the machine rocked back and forth, then steadied.

Alex dared not move. The caterpillar tracks were still jammed on the splintered branch, but the slightest vibration could tip the fragile balance. Then the snowmobile would complete its plunge into the icy water and he and Amber would be swept under the ice to their deaths.

Behind him Amber was shuddering with cold and fear.

'Amber, can you hear me?' said Alex, without turning round.

'Yeah,' said Amber in a trembling voice.

'Try to stay very still,' said Alex. 'The others will get us out.'

On cue, a torch beam shone down on them.

On the lip of the suck hole, Li felt her heart sink as she moved the torch, concentrating the beam first on the ski tips of the fallen snowmobile, then on the caterpillar tracks clinging to the splintered branch. Hex hurried up beside her, then flung himself down on the snow and stretched his arm into the suck hole, trying to reach Amber.

'No point,' said Li briefly. Her years of free climbing had given her the ability to judge distances with great accuracy and she could see that there was no way they could stretch far enough to reach Alex and Amber.

Hex scrambled to his feet again. His green eyes were wild behind his goggles. 'What then?' he snapped.

'Ropes,' said Li. 'Paulo!' she called. 'We need—'

She stopped as Paulo came up beside them, dragging two lengths of strong nylon cord. He had already unhooked the trailers from two of the snowmobiles and tied the other end of each rope to the back of the machines.

'Li, Hex,' said Paulo, making a lasso out of the rope ends. 'You must go to your snowmobiles and get ready to pull them out.'

Li and Hex ran to the machines, scrambled on and revved their engines, looking back at Paulo for the signal to go. Paulo called down into the suck hole.

'Amber? Alex? I am going to throw you a rope each. Catch the loop and slip it over your arms and head.'

'Right,' called Alex, not daring to raise his head to look at Paulo.

A second later, the rope came hurtling down towards Amber. She reached out and grabbed it. Alex's rope came next. He tried to grab it but it was just too far ahead of him. His rope swung out of reach and hit the side of the suck hole.

'Do not worry,' called Paulo, hauling in the rope. 'I will throw again.'

'Amber,' said Alex as he waited for his rope to fall again, 'get that rope around you.'

'Already there.'

'OK. Good girl.'

Paulo threw the rope again and this time Alex managed to grab it but, as he did so, he jerked forward slightly. The movement was enough to dislodge the tips of the snowmobile skis, and with a scraping like nails on a blackboard they began to judder down the ice wall. Alex had no time to slip the rope around his chest. Instead, as the nose of the snowmobile dipped towards the water, he quickly slipped his arm through the lasso, then flicked the rope a few times so that it formed loops around his wrist and arm.

'Go! Go!' yelled Paulo. Li and Hex leaned forward on their machines and opened the throttles. The ropes uncoiled behind them and twanged into a quivering straight line. The machines jerked backwards and the caterpillar tracks struggled to retain their grip on the ice, then, slowly, they began moving forward again.

In the suck hole, the snowmobile skis lost their grip and the machine plunged down into the water. As Alex fell with the machine, he gripped the rope hard and prayed that the lasso would tighten around his arm and hold him up. Above him, Amber was jerked from the back of the snowmobile by the rope around her chest. She slammed against the ice wall and the rope began to pull her up the side of the hole. Alex hit the water and disappeared.

The snowmobile was sucked under the ice, and in an instant it had whirled away into the blackness. Alex's hand let go of the rope when he hit the freezing water. He could not help it. His muscles, his lungs, his whole body was stunned by the shock of the icy water. He felt the current take him and he began to whirl away under the ice after the snowmobile. Then Paulo's lasso tightened around his wrist. A massive pain ripped through his shoulder as the rope yanked him to a stop. For a few seconds he hung just below the ice, strung out on the end of the rope in the strong current like a kite on the wind. Then the rope began to drag him back towards the bottom of the suck hole.

Alex was in agony. His shoulder felt as though it was full of broken glass, all his muscles were cramping and every centimetre of skin burned with a cold fire. The icy water had acted like a punch in the guts, sending his diaphragm into spasm, which at least meant that his lungs had not flooded with water.

His outstretched arm reached the bottom of the suck hole and began to twist as the rope dragged it upwards, bending it back on to the slope of the wall. His shoulder rotated and the pain increased as the angle got more extreme, until he thought he was going to pass out. Then his shoulder joint popped out of its socket. For two seconds Alex's dislocated arm bent back further than any arm should go and then, finally, the rest of his body came out of the water and he was dragged up the side of the suck hole.

For a time, Alex drifted in and out of consciousness. He was aware of being stripped of his clothes and rubbed dry. The next time he came to, he was zipped up inside one of the sleeping bags and riding side-saddle on Paulo's snowmobile. His head was resting against Paulo's chest and Paulo's arms were braced on either side of him, holding his shivering body in place and steering the machine at the same time. Alex raised his head and looked groggily up at Paulo.

'Does this mean we're going steady?' he said through chattering teeth.

Paulo grinned down at him, then the snowmobile began to jolt as it reached the pressure ridges at the edge of the river. The pain blossomed in Alex's shoulder again and he sank back into darkness.

Paulo's smile disappeared as he concentrated on steering his snowmobile over the ridges and up the side of the river bank. He had spotted a stand of trees on the bank where they could build Alex a bed of spruce boughs and light a fire to warm him up. He knew they had to move fast. There was a basic rule for warming up someone suffering from hypothermia. If they cooled down slowly, they must be warmed up slowly. If they cooled down fast, they must be warmed up fast. Alex's core temperature had been reduced by a drastic amount in just a few seconds of immersion and now his face was blue with cold. It was crucial to get a fire going as soon as possible.

Paulo reached the top of the bank and headed for the trees. Amber and Li followed on the second snowmobile and Hex brought up the rear on the third machine. Once they reached the trees, they moved with an organized urgency, and in a very short time Alex was lying on a bed of spruce boughs in front of a roaring fire. They had opened the side zip of the sleeping bag so that the warmth of the flames could reach him, and gradually his shudders were lessening and his skin was pinking up.

'What now?' asked Amber, staring at Alex's pale face.

'Now,' said Paulo grimly, 'I must put his shoulder back into place. The dislocated bone may be pressing on nerves or blood vessels. I must remove the pressure to restore circulation to the arm and prevent permanent nerve damage. I must do it now. The longer I wait, the more swollen the area will become and the more difficult it will be to put the bone back into the socket.'

The others nodded their agreement. They trusted Paulo. He was the group's medic and he had a sure, steady hand when dealing with injuries. He had learned how to tend the wounds of both cattle and men on the long treks to the further reaches of his family ranch back in Argentina.

Alex came to again, groaning with pain as Paulo bent over him, gently probing the dislocated shoulder.

'Alex, listen to me,' said Paulo.

Alex opened his eyes and focused on Paulo's serious face.

'Good. Alex, your shoulder is dislocated. I must put the bone back into the socket for you.'

'OK,' muttered Alex.

Paulo hesitated, then decided it would be best to prepare Alex. 'It will hurt,' he said.

'A lot?' asked Alex.

'Yes. I am sorry. Are you ready?'

Alex gritted his teeth and closed his eyes. 'Go on,' he said.

Paulo nodded to Hex, who was kneeling on Alex's other side. Hex held Alex down and Paulo removed his mukluk and pressed his heel into Alex's armpit. Bracing his leg, he gripped Alex's arm and pulled it out straight, exerting a steady pressure on the shoulder joint. Alex screamed with pain and bucked, trying to shake Hex off him. Hex lay over Alex's chest and Paulo pulled until the sweat popped out on his forehead.

'Stop it!' shouted Amber as Alex screamed again. 'It's not working! You're just hurting him!'

Then Alex's shoulder joint finally slid over the rim of the socket and settled back into place with an audible click. Immediately, Paulo released the pressure and gently lowered Alex's arm to his chest.

'You weren't kidding,' said Alex, his voice weak and trembling.

'Sorry,' said Paulo again.

Amber brought Alex a hot drink and some painkillers to take, and at last the pain dulled and he slept.

'That is good,' said Paulo. 'That is what he needs now. We shall build up the fire and wait—'

'Shhh!' interrupted Li. She had heard something. As they all listened, it came again, drifting across the frozen landscape. It was the long, mournful howl of a wolf.

Eleven

The sound made all the hairs on the back of Amber's neck rise in a shivering line.

'Is that what I think it is?' she asked, gazing wide-eyed at Li.

'A wolf?' asked Li. 'Yes it is.'

'Oh, that's just great,' quavered Amber.

'But that wolf, he is very far away. Yes?' asked Paulo.

Li nodded in agreement.

'So, there is no danger—'

Paulo broke off as another, answering howl

trembled through the cold air. This one was closer. A lot closer.

'I knew I was right to hate this place,' muttered Hex, searching the darkening skyline.

'Don't worry,' said Li. 'A wolf pack hunts by picking off the sick, old or wounded animals from a herd. They won't go for a group of humans unless—'

'Unless what?' demanded Amber.

'Unless they're desperately hungry – and that's not very likely right at the start of winter.'

Amber relaxed, then tensed again as she heard something on the frozen river. Her eyes widened as she identified the sound. It was claws scratching on ice. The scratching grew louder, accompanied by loud panting and the occasional yipping bark. The pack was racing along the frozen river and drawing closer by the second.

Without a word, Amber, Hex, Li and Paulo each picked a flaming branch from the fire and moved into a protective semicircle around Alex. They waited, hoping against hope that the pack would carry on down the river and pass them by. That did not happen. The scratching of claws changed to a scrabbling as the beasts swerved up on to the bank, and a second later the leader surged over the top of the bank and raced towards them, closely followed by the rest of the pack.

Amber screamed at the sight of the glinting teeth and lolling tongues. Then she screamed again as she saw a much bigger beast coming after the pack.

'It's OK!' shouted Li, suddenly realizing what she was seeing. 'It's not wolves! It's a dog team and sled.'

Amber sagged with relief as the driver shouted, 'Whoa!' at the same time as slamming his foot down on a steel claw between the runners. The claw dug down into the snow, the team slowed and the sled came to a halt. The driver stepped down from the back of the sled and walked towards them, loosening the drawstrings on his fur-trimmed hood.

Hex stiffened and raised his flaming branch again. It had just occurred to him that this man might not be friendly. He scanned the man's clothes for any sign of an Usher Mining Corporation logo, but there was nothing to be seen. The man pushed his hood back to reveal a round, friendly Inuit face, split in a smile.

'We thought they were wolves,' explained Amber, lowering her own branch.

'There is some wolf in 'em,' said the man, waving a mittened hand at his team. 'Some husky. Some other breeds too. They're a real mixture.'

'We heard a wolf howling,' said Paulo. 'It was very close.'

The man shook his head. 'It was much further away than it sounded. Those wolf howls can carry ten miles or more.'

'What do you want?' said Hex, still suspicious.

'Saw your fire,' said the man. 'Stopped off to say hello. My name is Amaruk.' He turned to Amber with a mischievous glint in his eyes. 'It means wolf.'

Amber smiled. 'My name's—'

'Amber,' said Amaruk and he laughed when her mouth dropped open in surprise. 'Am I right?'

'How did you know that?' squeaked Amber.

'I'm a friend of Papaluk's,' explained Amaruk. 'She told me you'd be heading my way this week, so I've been keeping an eye out for you.'

'You know Papaluk?' asked Li, stepping forward.

'Yeah. I'm heading out to the bay now, just to make

sure she's OK. I heard there's been some kinda trouble there. The supply plane pilots found a body or something.'

Li and Hex shared a look but Amaruk didn't see it. He had spotted Alex, lying in front of the fire, with his bandaged shoulder sticking out of the sleeping bag. 'Hey, is he hurt? What happened here?'

'Amaruk,' said Li quietly, 'I have some bad news.'

She took Amaruk to one side to tell him about Papaluk. Amber, Hex and Paulo remained by the fire, watching as Amaruk's shoulders slumped and Li rested a hand on his arm. The dogs seemed to know something was wrong. They had been lolling in the snow but now they sat up and looked towards their master, whining and yipping.

When Li and Amaruk had finished talking, they returned to the fire. Amaruk was no longer smiling. 'Sounds like you've all had quite a time of it,' he said, squatting by the fire. 'Papaluk said you were into extreme sports, but what you've just been through is so extreme, most folks would be dead by now.' He looked at each of them in turn, and his gaze was shrewd and considering. 'Who are you kids?' he asked quietly. 'And what's really going on here?'

'What do you mean?' asked Hex, returning Amaruk's gaze with a bland stare.

'OK,' said Amaruk. 'If that's how you want to play it. Just give me a minute, will you?' He stared into the flames for a long time. Finally, he roused himself and stared up at the threatening sky. A cloud bank had rolled in overhead and the wind was rising.

'Storm on the way,' he said briefly. 'I can't help Papaluk now, but I can help her friends, whatever you're up to. Come on. I'll take you back to my village. It's on the banks of the river, not far away. The mine you were looking for is just a bit further on. A lot of the guys in the village used to work there, before Usher took it over.'

As they created a bed for Alex on Amaruk's sled, the first snow began to fall. By the time Alex was strapped securely in place, they were in the middle of a blizzard. Mean, hard pellets of snow were blowing almost horizontally on a rising wind.

'Maybe we should camp up until this is over!' yelled Hex.

Amaruk shook his head as he strapped a headlamp around his forehead and clipped the battery pack to his belt. 'We need to get Alex here into a warm bed as soon as possible.'

'But you can't see more than two metres in front of you in this!'

'Don't need to,' said Amaruk, ruffling the thick fur of his lead dog. 'I've got Boomer.' He looked down at the dog and it gazed back adoringly, leaning in against his leg. It was a big male with black, tan and white markings and a tail that curled over its back like a question mark. 'Boomer's short for Boomerang, because he always finds his way back. We've been together a long time, me and Boomer. He's brought me home through much worse than this.'

'What if we come across another suck hole?' asked Amber fearfully. The terrifying experience of falling into the ice funnel was still fresh in her mind.

'If you'd been travelling with dogs,' said Amaruk, 'you would never have fallen in. They would've taken you right around it. They can sense weak ice or open water.'

Amber looked admiringly at Boomer. What she had just heard reinforced all her prejudices about using machines for transport. 'I could really get to like these guys,' she grinned.

'Stay close on my tail and keep your eyes on this light,' said Amaruk, turning his headband round until the lamp sat on the back of his hood.

'Don't you need to see where you're going?' asked Amber.

'I have Boomer,' said Amaruk simply, slotting his mukluks into the rubber footprints on the back of his sled. 'Headlights on and stay in single file. Follow the sled tracks exactly. The dogs know the safe ice. And keep a check on one another to make sure no-one falls behind.' Alpha Force nodded, pulled their hood drawstrings tight and clambered on to their machines, with Amber and Li sharing the third one. Amaruk tightened his own fur-fringed hood until only his eyes were showing, then pulled the sled brake out of the snow and yelled to his dogs, 'Let's go!'

They followed Amaruk's bobbing lamp through the whirling snow for twenty freezing minutes before the dogs began to yelp with excitement. Li peered through her snow-covered goggles and saw the faintest glimmer of lights. They had arrived in Amaruk's village. Boomer had guided them home.

'It's a proper house,' said Amber a few minutes later, as she followed Amaruk up the steps and into a warm, wooden-floored hallway. Through an open doorway she could see a family living room with a sofa and chairs, prints and photographs on the walls and two children sitting in front of a television in the corner.

'Yeah, well, we tried getting all our furniture into the igloo, but it wouldn't fit,' said a slim, pretty Inuit woman, emerging from the kitchen. She had dancing black eyes, high, flat cheekbones and thick, black hair done up in two plaits.

'I'm sorry,' said Amber, squirming with embarrassment. 'I only meant—'

'And I'm only teasing,' smiled the woman, turning to give Amaruk a kiss on the cheek.

'This is Kikik, my wife,' said Amaruk.

Li staggered up the steps and ripped off her

goggles. Her left eye was closed and she had to use her fingers to prise it open. Her eyelashes had frozen and stuck together like glue. 'I've never known cold like it!' she stuttered through stiff lips.

'It's the wind chill factor,' said Kikik.

'It can get a lot worse than that,' boasted Amaruk. 'I've known it so cold you could spit and it would freeze in mid-air and bounce when it hit the ground.'

'Mind your backs,' grunted Hex as he and Paulo staggered into the hallway, carrying Alex. He was sitting between them on their crossed and linked arms, still bundled up in his sleeping bag like a caterpillar.

'This is Alex,' said Amaruk. 'He fell through the ice.'

Kikik thumped Amaruk on the chest. 'Standing there chatting! Why didn't you tell me?'

'I just did,' said Amaruk.

Instantly Kikik was all seriousness, leading Hex and Paulo through into a bedroom at the end of the hallway, then shooing them out again once Alex was laid on the bed.

'Don't worry,' said Amaruk, as they all stared anxiously at the closed bedroom door. 'Kikik is a nurse. Now, come and meet my boys, Pungar and Ohoto.'

Two young Inuit boys, aged five and seven, immediately turned off the television and scrambled to their feet to greet their guests.

'Would you like some akutug?' asked Ohoto politely.

'Akutug?' repeated Amber.

'It's Inuit ice cream,' explained Amaruk. 'A traditional delicacy.'

'Oh. OK,' said Amber, and the two little boys ran giggling from the room and came back a few minutes later with four bowls of what looked like fluffy sorbet topped with red berries.

'This looks good,' said Paulo, taking a bowl. Amber, Li and Hex all took a bowl too and, with the boys watching their every move, they popped a big spoonful of the sorbet into their mouths. The boys could barely contain themselves as they watched their four guests struggle not to show how bad the taste was. Paulo and Li swallowed their mouthfuls down in one gulp. This was an Inuit delicacy and they did not want to insult their hosts. Hex thought about swallowing his mouthful, but his stomach heaved at the idea. He looked from side to side like a hunted animal and spat his mouthful back into the bowl. Amber froze with her cheeks bulging and her eyes growing wide, then she opened her mouth and scraped the stuff off her tongue with the spoon.

'OK. Joke over,' smiled Amaruk. 'Time for bed. It's a school day tomorrow.'

The boys ran from the room, shrieking with laughter.

'We are sorry,' began Paulo.

'Don't be. It's fine not to like it,' said Amaruk. 'Inuit ice cream is a bit of an acquired taste.'

'What's in it?' shuddered Amber, pushing her bowl as far away from her as she could manage.

'A mixture of seal oil, caribou fat, sugar and water,' grinned Amaruk.

'Yummy,' muttered Hex.

'Do your boys like it?' asked Li.

'Hell, no! Ben and Jerry's is their favourite. They just like to torment our guests from the south. I run a tour business, you see. Arctos Tours. We fly the people in here, then take them out on the sleds for a couple of weeks. They learn how to drive the teams, fish in the frozen lakes, camp out in the wilderness and breathe a bit of clean air for a change. Most people love it. Apart from the Inuit ice cream, that is. Years ago, they used to call it Eskimo ice cream, but that's kinda frowned upon now.'

'Why?' asked Hex.

'Well, Eskimo is a Cree Indian name for us. It means, "eaters of raw flesh". It used to be a pretty accurate description, I suppose. My people used to eat all their meat raw because it saved on fuel and it was a valuable source of vitamins. That was important when the only other sources used to be a few berries and roots in the summer. Nowadays, we get our vegetables flown in and we all have generators in our houses. We still eat raw meat dishes sometimes, on special occasions, but we prefer to be called Inuit now. It's our own word. It means "the people".'

Kikik came into the room and smiled around at the four members of Alpha Force. 'Alex is going to be just fine,' she said. 'His temperature's nearly back up to normal already and there's no sign of frostbite. As for the shoulder, the swelling isn't too bad at all. No lasting damage. I've strapped it up and given him some anti-inflammatories and painkillers. He's sleeping now.'

'Was it good?' asked Paulo hesitantly. 'What I did for his arm?'

'You did a great job, Paulo,' smiled Kikik. 'Now, would somebody like to tell me what's going on?'

Amaruk took his wife by the hand and looked up into her face. 'Papaluk has walked upon the land,' he said softly. He was referring to the old Inuit tradition of walking out into the snow when you were too old or sick to live usefully any more. It was his way of breaking the news of Papaluk's death gently.

Kikik's eyes filled with tears and she cried for her friend. Amber cried too, but Li sat stony-faced, waiting for the right moment to ask her question. As soon as Amaruk had finished explaining what had happened to Papaluk, Li jumped in.

'Amaruk, you said the mine wasn't far from here.'

'You can reach it in a morning's travel.'

'Why do you want to go there?' asked Kikik.

'Papaluk had proof that the mine was dumping cyanide into the river. That's why Daniel Usher had her killed. He doesn't know we're on his trail. If we can get into the mine while he's feeling safe, the chances are we're going to find enough evidence to put him away for a good long time.'

'Our water is piped up from the river,' said Kikik. 'It used to be the purest water you could wish for. Since Usher Mining Corporation took over the mine, we have had sickness here. There is a pattern to it. For a week, maybe two, everything is fine. Then within one day, people come into the surgery reporting all sorts of symptoms. Headaches, vertigo, nausea and vomiting. The little children are brought in with dilated pupils and clammy skin. Some even have convulsions.'

'They must be the dumping days,' said Hex.

Kikik nodded. 'Mostly the people recover and then everyone is fine again until the next time. But now – now a young woman in the village has given birth to a baby with bad problems. Everyone is scared. We are all melting snow for our cooking and having bottled water flown in to drink. I looked up our symptoms on the Net and they all fit the cyanide poisoning profile.'

'That's why we have to nail this guy,' said Amber.

'But why you? Why must you go to the mine?' asked Amaruk. 'It will be risky.'

'Because it's personal. Papaluk was my friend,' said Li.

'And Daniel Usher had my parents killed,' said Amber quietly.

'And we are —' Hex hesitated – 'experienced – in this sort of stuff.'

There was a long silence. Amaruk and Kikik looked at the four fit and muscular young people sitting in their living room. Amaruk opened his mouth to ask what Hex meant, but Hex was watching him with a cool stare and a neutral, closed expression on his face and Amaruk decided against the question.

Amaruk and Kikik shared a look, then Amaruk seemed to make a decision. 'Papaluk was our friend too,' he said. 'I'll guide you to the mine. But you'd better leave the snowmobiles here. The mine's very well guarded and they might investigate if they hear you coming. We'll use the dog teams.'

Li looked around at the others and they all nodded their agreement. 'Good,' she said. 'We leave tomorrow.'

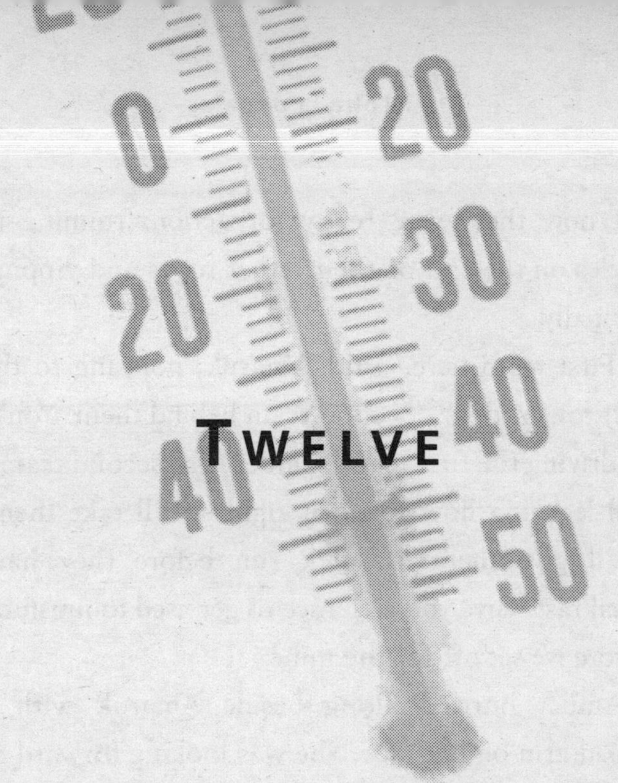

Twelve

'There they are,' said Amaruk the next morning. 'Sixteen dogs. Two teams.'

Amber, Hex, Li and Paulo looked out over the crisp, new snow. The blizzard had subsided during the night and the day was bright and clear, but they could see no sign of the dogs.

'Where?' demanded Amber.

Amaruk gave a high, clear whistle and suddenly sixteen dogs exploded out of the ground. They had all been curled up under a blanket of snow, with their paws and noses tucked neatly under their tails, but now they were ready for action, running in circles on the end of their tether ropes and yipping excitedly.

'First team here,' said Amaruk, pointing to the first row of dogs. 'Second team behind them. You'll be driving the first team, Amber. The second team's still learning how to do it right so I'll take them. We'll give them a quick run before they have breakfast. Give you a chance to get used to mushing before we set off for the mine.'

Amber hurried along beside Amaruk with a broad grin on her face. She was looking forward to this. When Amaruk had explained that they would have to take two sleds as each one carried a maximum of three people, including the driver, she had instantly volunteered to be the second driver.

Amaruk pulled the covering from his two sleds and began yanking one of them back and forth to break the runners out of the ice.

'I can see why we need two sleds,' said Paulo, grabbing the other sled and copying Amaruk's technique. 'They are not very big.'

The sleds were lightweight baskets made out of

lashed hickory. They were attached to long runners made of tough polyethylene plastic which had been polished until it was as smooth as glass. At the rear of the sled, the frame rose up into a curved handlebar. Behind the handlebar, a pair of rubber footprints were set into a plate where the driver, known as the musher, stood.

The dogs grew even more frenzied as Amaruk and Paulo pushed the sleds across the snow towards them.

'Are they friendly?' asked Hex, watching the dogs warily.

'Most of them,' said Amaruk, picking a tangle of harnesses from the sled. 'Come on, I'll introduce you as we harness them up.'

Amaruk selected a long length of nylon rope just over a centimetre in diameter. 'This is called the gangline,' he said as he attached the rope to the front of the sled, then laid the length of it out along the snow. 'It's the main line. You attach all your dogs to the gangline in staggered pairs, using these.'

He held up eight short lengths of rope, each half a centimetre in diameter. 'These are the tuglines and they clip on to the dog's harness. See?' Amaruk picked up a harness and showed them the metal ring on the padded straps. 'The dog's front legs go through these side loops here and the straps transfer the strain of pulling to the dog's chest and shoulders. That's partly why a team of eight can pull a weight of three hundred kilos without even breaking into a sweat.'

'And those? What are they?' asked Paulo, pointing to a pile of even shorter, thinner ropes.

'They're the necklines. They don't do anything except keep your dogs in line once they're on the move. Right, let's go harness them up.' Amaruk handed the tuglines to Amber and picked up the harnesses.

'You've met Boomer already,' he said, stopping by the first dog in the line and bending to slip on the harness. Boomer licked Amaruk on the cheek and he ruffled the dog's fur in return. 'He's my lead dog. I've had him since he was a pup and sometimes I think he can read my mind.'

Amaruk led Boomer over to the front of the gangline and clipped his tugline into place. 'Come and meet the others,' he said.

The next dog was a friendly little female with fluffy, white fur. 'This here is Pie,' said Amaruk.

'Why did you call her Pie?' asked Li, watching as Amber harnessed the dog with surprising skill and speed considering that she had never done it before.

'Because she's as nice as pie,' said Amaruk. 'Not a leader, though. She has to have someone to follow and she'd follow Boomer anywhere. She's a second lead. A stringer. Moving on, this is Donald.'

'Why Donald?' asked Paulo, as the third dog was harnessed up. At that moment, Donald gave a strangled yelp of excitement as his tether rope was unclipped. It sounded exactly like the quack of a duck. 'Never mind,' grinned Paulo.

'This is Frodo,' said Amaruk, petting a small male with big eyes, pointed ears and a lot of curly, dark hair. 'Because he's little but courageous. He shares swing position with Donald. Next we have Drum. He loves to roll in the snow. Drum roll. Get it? And this is Beauty, for obvious reasons. They take third pair position.'

Drum and Beauty were clipped into their places on the gangline. Now only two dogs were left still tethered to their sleeping posts. They were both big males with powerful shoulders and well-developed muscles in their back legs.

'These two are my wheel dogs,' explained Amaruk. 'Wheel dogs have to be big, tough brutes. They're the dogs closest to the sled, and when the musher makes a turn, most of the weight of the sled falls on their tuglines. This one is Stinker,' he said, harnessing a big, rangy dog with oatmeal-coloured fur and a laughing face. 'If you want to know why we call him Stinker, just sit next to him while he digests his dinner and you'll soon find out.' Amaruk handed Stinker's tugline to Paulo. 'And finally, we have Ice. He's my only Siberian husky. Cost me a fortune. I thought he would make a good leader but it didn't work out. We call him Ice, because he's very cool. He never really took to me, or anybody else, and you can't have a lead dog who doesn't care whether his musher lives or dies. He's a bit of a handful to harness up—'

Amaruk turned towards Ice, then stopped talking and stared in astonishment. Amber had already harnessed the big dog and was now sitting in the snow next to him, stroking his thick coat. Ice was leaning up against her, with one paw on her knee and an uncharacteristically soft look in his pale blue eyes.

'Well, I'll be . . . !' exclaimed Amaruk. 'I'd better qualify that last statement. Ice doesn't like people, unless their name happens to be Amber. He's taken a real shine to you, Amber. I've never seen him snuggle up to anyone like that before. I've heard mushers talk about dogs who only ever take to one person and when they do, they take to them within seconds. Looks like Ice here is a one-person dog – and he's just found his person.'

Amber grinned up at Amaruk and buried her fingers in the thick ruff of fur around Ice's neck.

'Come on then,' said Amaruk. 'Clip him in line. Then you can take them for a spin.'

Amber put Ice into his place then clambered up on to the back of the sled.

'Memorized the commands?' asked Amaruk.

Amber nodded. '"Let's go" to get them started. "Hike" to make them go faster. "Haw" for turn left, "gee" for turn right and "on by" to go straight on. "Easy" to slow them down and "whoa" for stop.'

'Good. Remember, you steer the sled by leaning one way or the other. The sharper the turn, the further you lean.'

Amber nodded again and released the claw brake. Taking a deep breath, she yelled out the musher's command, 'Let's go!'

The team shot off like a cork from a champagne bottle. Amber flew through the air and landed flat on her back as the sled was yanked from under her.

'Oww,' she said quietly, from the ground.

'Haw!' yelled Amaruk. 'Haw!'

Boomer heard him and turned the team to the left in a long curve until they were heading back towards Amaruk. 'On by!' called Amaruk, and Boomer obediently came out of the turn and headed straight on. 'Easy!' called Amaruk as the sled drew closer. Then, 'Whoa!'

The sled came to a gentle halt at his feet. He held his hand out to Amber and pulled her up. 'Try again,' he said. 'And hold on tighter this time.'

'I'm not sure I can do it,' whispered Amber, her cheeks burning with embarrassment.

'Course you can. The dogs like you. That's the most important thing. They're keen to do as you want. You just have to learn how to tell them what you want.'

Amber sighed and climbed back on. Over the next hour she tipped the sled over twice and fell off three times. The fourth time she fell, she flung out her hand and grabbed the sled, determined to hang on. She bounced along on her front for a good two minutes, with the dogs heading for the far horizon, before she remembered to shout, 'Whoa!'

When she returned, Hex, Li and Paulo were so weak with laughter, they could hardly stand.

'Why don't you boys leave us to get on with this,' said Amaruk, seeing the look in Amber's eyes.

'What about me?' asked Li.

'I think you should stick around,' said Amaruk. 'You're small but strong. You'd make a good musher.'

'Yeah!' grinned Amber. 'Stay and keep me company, Li! It's about time someone else fell on their ass for a change.'

While Li climbed on to the back of the sled to take her turn as musher, Paulo and Hex stumbled off to explore the village, still shuddering with the occasional convulsion of laughter and clinging to one another for support. There wasn't a lot to see. At the centre of the village there was a small school, which doubled as a surgery and village hall. Clustered around the school was a collection of brightly painted wooden houses on stilts, each with its own fuel tank, radio mast and string of dogs outside. In a country with hardly any roads, everyone used snowmobiles, dog teams or small planes to get around.

Ohoto and Pungar spotted them through the schoolroom windows and dragged Paulo into the building to meet their friends. Hex had arranged to call in on Kikik with his camcorder. She took him to see the young woman and her sick baby. The sad-faced woman gave him permission to film them, once Kikik explained that Hex was building up a record of evidence against Usher Mining Corporation. By the time Hex returned to Amaruk's house, all the laughter had drained out of him.

He found Amber, Li and Paulo standing by the two loaded sleds, while Amaruk made last-minute checks on the harnesses.

'Come on, Hex!' yelled Amber. 'We're ready to move out! Amaruk finally gave me the thumbs-up. I can drive the sled! Do you want to ride with me?'

Hex groaned. 'I'd rather live a bit longer,' he said.

'Suit yourself.' Amber looked at Li, then Paulo, but they both suddenly became very interested in their feet.

'Well somebody has to!' exploded Amber.

'I will,' said a voice behind them.

They turned to see Alex standing on the house steps. Kikik had dried all his clothes and he was fully dressed. One jacket sleeve hung loose and empty, but that was the only sign of the ordeal Alex had suffered the previous day. Otherwise he looked as fit and healthy as ever.

'You cannot travel yet,' protested Paulo.

'Yes I can,' said Alex, not quite managing to hide a wince as he stepped down on to the snow. 'My shoulder's hardly hurting now and I've got my drugs here.'

'But—'

'You're not stopping me,' said Alex, clambering into Amber's sled, his grey eyes steely with determination.

The others knew there would be no arguing with him in this mood. Amaruk opened his mouth to say something, then he closed it again. If Alex felt strong enough to travel, then he was not going to fight with the boy. Kikik would have his hide for taking her patient off for a sled ride, but he would weather that storm when it came.

'Stubborn as a mule,' muttered Hex, giving Alex a glare before clambering on to the sled behind him.

Li and Paulo climbed on to Amaruk's sled and Amaruk and Amber took their places as mushers.

'Ready?' called Amber. 'Let's go!'

THIRTEEN

The dogs flattened out, running hard, and the sled runners hissed through the fresh snow. They raced down to the frozen river and turned on to the ice, side by side. The sled runners grated over the pressure ridges, then they were out on to the smooth ice in the middle and heading upriver towards the mine. Amber watched her dogs and noticed that, on their left sides, where the slanting sun touched them, there was no sign of frost, but the thick fur on their shadowed sides glittered with tiny ice crystals, even after an hour of running. It was an exhilarating way to travel, and when Amaruk called a halt for food after two hours, Amber was reluctant to stop.

While Hex and Li went up on to the bank to collect wood for a fire, Paulo used the hand-operated ice drill to make a hole through the ice. Alex handed over the fishing hooks and lines from his survival tin and watched from the sled as Paulo caught six good-sized walleye and pike in quick succession.

'They are jumping out of the water!' he cried, grinning at Alex.

'I know how they feel,' muttered Alex, shuddering at the memory of the freezing water under the ice.

He threw his knife to Paulo, who used it to gut the fish before threading them on to sticks ready for grilling. The fish guts were added to the bucketful of dry dog food, seal meat and fat cakes that Amber and Amaruk were feeding to the dogs.

Hex and Li returned with a good pile of fuel, and within five minutes the fire was lit and the fish were grilling.

'Not bad. Not bad at all,' said Amaruk, looking around approvingly as he put a bucket of snow next to the fire to melt for the dogs' drinking water. 'You work well together.'

As soon as the dogs had been watered and Alex had taken his next dose of painkillers and anti-inflammatories, Alpha Force cleared the temporary camp and clambered back on to the sleds. They were anxious to get to the mine while there was still some daylight. Amber urged her dogs on, calling out the musher commands with increasing confidence. She was mystified and more than a little disappointed when her team suddenly skidded to an unauthorized halt.

'Let's go!' called Amber, but the dogs would not move. They danced in place on the ice, whining softly and sending nervous glances towards the stand of spruce trees on the near bank to their right.

'There must be something up there,' said Alex, peering into the darkness between the trees.

'Amaruk's team went past without a problem,' said Amber.

'But they were much further over to the left,' said Alex.

Papaluk's tranquillizer rifle was tucked into the

sled by his leg. He reached under his blankets and eased the weapon half out of its holster. He was not even sure whether he could fire the rifle one-handed, but the behaviour of the dogs was making him nervous and the rifle stock felt reassuringly solid under his hand.

Up ahead, Amaruk stopped and jammed the snow-hook brake into the ice to hold his team. He clambered from the sled and walked back towards Amber.

'I'll see if I can lead them past,' decided Amber, climbing from the sled and walking forward.

'Wait!' called Amaruk. 'Let me check the ice. They may have sensed a weakness.'

Amaruk and Amber moved slowly towards one another with their heads down, staring at the ice. But Amaruk was wrong. The ice was not where the danger lay. If they had looked up at the trees, they would have seen death hurtling down the bank towards them.

The moose is the largest member of the deer family. Solitary and fiercely territorial, a single animal can eat up to twenty kilos of vegetation a day and needs a large area of land to support it. A big bull moose can stand two and a half metres high and weigh up to eight hundred kilos.

This one was a monster. It careered down the bank towards Amber and Amaruk, bellowing with rage and lowering its heavy, flattened antlers. Its territory had been invaded and it was going in for the attack.

Amber stared at the huge moose charging down on her. She was frozen with fear. She had always thought of a moose as a slightly comical animal, with its long face and bulbous nose, but this was the first time she had come face to face with a charging bull. The lethal antlers had a spread of over two metres and the pointed hooves cut deep gouges in the ice as the moose reached the river and powered towards her.

Hex leaped from his place behind Alex and began running towards Amber. Li and Paulo had left the front sled and were running back, but Hex could see that none of them were going to reach Amber in time.

'Amber!' he yelled, and the desperation in his voice brought her out of her frightened trance. She started to run, but she was too late. There was not enough time left to get out of the way. Then Amaruk crashed into her side and rammed her out of the path of the huge beast. Amber went rolling away across the ice as Amaruk stumbled and fell on to his knees in front of Boomer. The moose changed direction slightly, heading for Amaruk.

In the sled, Alex had reacted quickly. As soon as he saw the charging moose, he had wrestled the tranquillizer rifle from its holster with his good arm and lifted the weapon to his shoulder. The rifle was primed with a tranquillizer dart, but Alex found it impossible to hold the long-barrelled weapon steady with one hand. Cursing, he dropped the rifle, tore open his jacket and yanked his other arm out of its sling. Wincing with pain, he lifted the rifle, two-handed this time, and took aim.

An instant later, the sled jerked forward and Alex was sent sprawling. As the bellowing moose prepared to ram the kneeling Amaruk, Boomer had leaped in front of his master with his teeth bared in a snarl. The beast's antlers hooked Boomer off the ice and sent him tumbling through the air. He screamed as he smacked down on to the hard surface again and skidded across the ice, jerking the other dogs and the sled after him.

The enraged moose charged after Boomer, catching Amaruk a glancing blow on the side of the head with its hoof as it passed him. Boomer tried to get out of the way but he was hopelessly entangled in the gangline. The moose reared over him and began to smash its sharp hooves down again and again. Boomer twisted back and forth to avoid being trampled, but each movement tangled him ever more tightly in the gangline.

Hex and Paulo pulled a dazed Amaruk out of the way and Li helped Amber to her feet as Alex once again lifted the rifle to his shoulder. The moose was just a few metres away from him, but it was rearing up, then smashing its hooves down on to the ice and sending shock waves shuddering through the sled. Added to that, the other dogs were scrabbling backwards to get away from the moose and jerking the sled along with them. Alex took a deep breath and concentrated on finding his mark.

As Alex took aim, Boomer's luck finally ran out. The moose came down on his hind leg. The sharp hooves split the leg open and the huge weight of the beast snapped the bone like a twig. Boomer screamed as blood began to pour from the wound.

'Hurry! Hurry!' sobbed Amber, as Boomer's scream echoed across the frozen river.

Alex's eyes narrowed. He squeezed the trigger and the tranquillizer dart hit the moose squarely in the side of the neck. The maddened beast did not feel the impact, but as the drug flooded its system, it stopped, staggered sideways and stood snorting with its head lowered. It took a few steps towards the bank, then its legs folded and it collapsed on to the ice.

Amaruk scrambled up and ran towards his lead dog. Boomer was panting with pain and fear, but he made a happy whine in his throat when he saw his master. He tried to struggle to his feet, but his injured leg would not work and he collapsed on to the ice again.

'All right, boy. All right,' whispered Amaruk, falling to his knees and easing the dog's head on to his lap. Boomer made the happy whine in his throat again and lifted his head. As Amaruk bent over him, he licked his master's face, then laid his head down and gave a tired sigh. His eyes fluttered closed and his body relaxed.

'He is going into shock,' said Paulo, crouching beside the wounded dog. 'And he is losing a lot of blood. We must stop the bleeding and keep him warm.'

While Paulo searched Amber's sled for the medical kit, Amaruk unharnessed Boomer and carried him over to his own sled. There, he laid the unconscious dog on a pure white polar bear skin and inspected the injury. Boomer's hind leg was twisted out of shape and his haunch muscle was sliced open in a long, curving line. Blood was soaking into the bearskin, but Amaruk was relieved to see that it was leaking steadily from the whole length of the wound rather than coming from one place in pulsing spurts.

'No major blood vessels torn,' he said, as Paulo hurried over with the medical kit.

'That is good,' said Paulo, sorting through the kit. He pushed aside Amber's spare insulin pens and pulled out a length of bandage. 'Now, we need two straight sticks.'

'I'll get those,' said Amber promptly. She had a good idea of what was going to happen next and she did not want to be around to see it.

'Alex, can you give Li one of your painkillers to crush?' asked Paulo as Amber and Hex hurried away to find the sticks.

Alex eased the little bottle of pills from his inside pocket, then handed Li his survival knife. 'Use the flat of the blade to crush the tablet,' he said.

Li nodded and set to work as Paulo looked over to Amaruk. 'Ready?' he asked.

Amaruk nodded, then took hold of Boomer around the hips, holding him steady. Paulo gripped the leg and eased the two ends of broken bone back into place. He did it as gently as he could but still the pain was severe enough to cause the unconscious dog to jerk and yowl deep in his throat. Paulo bit his lip but kept going until the leg was straight again. Quickly, he began to bandage the leg, and when

Amber and Hex hurried back with two straight sticks, he incorporated them into the bandage to act as splints.

When Paulo had finished, Amaruk took the knife with the powdered painkiller from Li. Gently, he eased open Boomer's jaws and shook the powdered drug on to the back of his tongue. Then he wrapped the dog up in the thick fur of the polar bear skin and made sure he was settled comfortably on the sled.

'Good dog,' he said. 'Good dog. You sleep well now.'

Scrubbing his nose with his mittened hand, Amaruk turned abruptly, walked back to Amber's sled and began to sort out the tangled lines. Amber hurried to help him.

'You'll have to choose a new lead dog,' he said, once the lines were straight again. 'Which one is it gonna be?'

Without hesitation, Amber walked to the back of the team and unhitched Ice from the gangline. He seemed to understand exactly what was happening and followed Amber to his new place at the front of the team, walking as proudly as a king. Pie whined as Ice was clipped to the gangline in front of her, but Ice turned on her with a snarl and she subsided obediently.

'Hmm,' said Amaruk. 'Looks promising. See how it goes, Amber. We should turn back,' he continued, as the rest of Alpha Force gathered round.

'No way,' said Amber. 'Daniel Usher killed my parents! We're not giving up now. We're going to that mine and collecting the evidence we need to convict him, even if we have to walk the rest of the way.'

Amber looked at the others and they all nodded their agreement.

'For Papaluk, too,' said Li. 'We have to do it for her.'

Amaruk looked around at their determined faces, then he sighed. He had not known Alpha Force for long, but already he knew that when they put on a united front like this, there was no arguing with them. 'OK. I'll take you to the mine, but then I must get Boomer back to the village. He saved my life just now. I have to do the same for him. Kikik will stitch him up and set the leg properly.' He looked around at Alpha Force. 'You sure you'll be OK at the mine?'

'No problem,' said Li. 'We'll sneak in the back way, collect our evidence and get out again. They won't even know we've been there.'

'No heroics?' said Amaruk.

'No heroics,' promised Hex.

Amaruk looked at them again, weighing up the options. He would never dream of leaving a bunch of ordinary kids alone in the wilds of northern Canada, but these were no ordinary kids. They were as capable of looking after themselves as any Inuit. 'OK,' he said finally. 'Let's get out of here before that moose wakes up again.'

The new sled team worked like a dream. Ice took to his new position as though he had been waiting all his life to be a lead dog. The other dogs were hesitant at first, but were soon following him without question. Amber had been running them slowly to start with, but once she saw that the formation was working, she called, 'Hike!' and the team surged forward. Amaruk matched her speed and the two sleds sped on upriver towards the mine.

Fourteen

'Not a pretty sight,' whispered Hex, panning the camcorder across the scene spread out below them. Alpha Force were lying in the snow at the top of a densely wooded ridge. Ahead of them, Daniel Usher's gold mine had gouged a huge, square scar out of the landscape. Behind them, the slope they had just climbed fell away steeply to the river.

Amaruk's mushing commands drifted up to them from the river, growing fainter by the second. He had taken his sled and set off to take Boomer home, promising to return that night to lead them back to the village. Amber's sled and team were still at the bottom of the ridge, hidden under the trees. As soon as Amber had embedded the snow-hook brake into the ground, the dogs had promptly dug holes in the snow, curled up and gone to sleep. Except for Ice. He sat like a dog made of stone, never taking his eyes from the place where Amber had disappeared and waiting for her return.

'I thought it would all be hidden underground,' gasped Amber, gazing over the top of the ridge at the raw devastation below.

'The old mine was,' explained Hex. 'But when all the richer seams of gold were worked out, Usher Mining started using the open cast method on the poorer grade ore.'

He pointed his camcorder at a deep pit on one side of the huge complex. 'That's where they quarry out the rock with explosives, then they use those big trucks to transport it to the leach pads down there.'

'Leach pads?' asked Li.

'Yeah. See all those square, murky-looking pools just below the ridge with the steam rising off them? They're full of crushed rock from the quarry.'

'I think they must be heated to stop them freezing over,' said Li, noting the generator at the edge of the pools.

'The dirty-looking liquid in them is sodium cyanide solution,' said Hex.

'Cyanide,' spat Li.

'It draws all the gold out of the rock, even particles too small for the naked eye to see. The trouble is, it also draws out any poisonous, heavy metals such as lead or mercury. Then the gold cyanide solution is piped into those sheds there, where they run it over carbon, which separates out all the gold.'

'And what do they do with the cyanide waste?' asked Paulo.

'According to what I read on the Net, it's supposed to be stored in specially lined vats, or recycled. But I don't think that's been happening here.' Hex shifted on to his other side and began filming the sheds. 'See how close the processing sheds are to the side of the ridge? The old mine workings go into the rock underneath us. My guess is that Usher Mining is dumping all the cyanide waste into the old mine workings. From there, it's trickling down through caves and tunnels in the rock and coming out at the bottom of the ridge on the other side, straight into the river.'

Alex finished his sweep with the binoculars and turned over on to his back to rest his injured shoulder more comfortably. 'They've got really good security,' he sighed. 'Perimeter fences, floodlights, security cameras, the lot. I counted ten guards around the processing sheds alone. You'd think there was gold in there,' he added wryly.

Paulo picked up the binoculars and studied the perimeter fence. 'We could cut that easily enough,' he said. 'It's not electrified.'

'Yes,' said Li. 'But look at the amount of open ground we'd have to cover once we were through. We'd be spotted in no time.'

'Maybe, if we worked out our hiding places in advance . . .' said Paulo, scanning the complex.

Alex shook his head. 'I already looked. Everything's too open. And after dark it's going to be lit up like a Christmas tree with all those floodlights. We're not going to get in that way without being seen.'

'We could come in through the quarry,' suggested Paulo. 'It all seems much quieter there.'

At that moment a red flag was hoisted in the quarry. Then a klaxon sounded, echoing around the bare rock walls. Seconds later, the ridge beneath them shuddered as an explosion ripped a slab of rock the size of a house away from the quarry wall. A huge plume of thick, brown dust rose into the air, then spread out over the quarry. The sound of the explosion reached them an instant after the ground shock, rumbling to a crescendo, then slowly fading.

'Much quieter, Paulo,' mocked Li.

Paulo grinned at her, then returned to his scan of the site. 'Wait a moment,' he said softly, focusing on the helicopter pad.

'What?' said Amber.

'There are two helicopters down there,' breathed Paulo. 'One is the standard issue company helicopter, for flying workers in and out. The other is a smaller, luxury helicopter. A private helicopter. It has the letters DU on the side.'

'Daniel Usher!' gasped Amber. 'He's here? The

big boss is right here at the mine?' She glared down at the helicopter pad and at the low, windowless building next to it, looking for a glimpse of the man who'd had her parents killed.

Li snatched the binoculars from Paulo. 'Looks like it,' she said, focusing on the private 'copter. 'That makes it even better. We sneak in, get our evidence and sneak out again, right under his nose.'

'Come on, guys,' said Amber, shuffling backwards away from the edge of the ridge. 'Plan B. We go in from the other side, at river level.'

They made their way back down the ridge to the sled. There, Amber and Hex changed into the two dry suits. They were the obvious choices for going into the cave system. Amber was the most experienced diver and Hex was in charge of the camcorder. Carrying the diving equipment, Alpha Force tramped along the river bank until they found a small opening at the base of the ridge. A stream of water was flowing out of the opening and disappearing under the ice into the river.

'This must be the place,' said Amber, checking the air flow from her tank. 'There's obviously an underground water system that the waste cyanide is feeding into.'

'What if it's contaminated?' said Li, gazing down at the water.

Hex snapped his gloves into place and checked the wrist seals on his dry suit. 'It looks clear enough. They're not dumping all the time, remember. Kikik said the poisoning symptoms only appeared every week or so.'

'But if that is only pure water,' said Paulo, 'then why has it not frozen like all the other water in this icicle of a country?'

'Because it's underground,' laughed Amber. 'Look, even if it is contaminated, we've got vulcanized rubber dry suits and full face masks. They'll keep out any contamination. Ready, Hex?'

Hex slung his underwater camcorder around his neck and turned on the lamp that was strapped to his head. 'Let's see what we can find.'

They stepped down into the stream, pushed their tanks through the small opening and squeezed through after them. They emerged into a narrow tunnel, with a shallow stream running along the bottom.

'Looks like it opens out at the end,' said Amber, as they both shone their lamps through the tunnel. Strapping on their tanks, they waded along the pebble and sand bottom of the stream. Amber could feel her heart beating fast. They each had a safety line around their waist, connecting them to the others on the river bank, and Amber could hear the lines slapping the surface of the water as Li and Paulo paid out the rope behind them. It was a reassuring sound, but ultimately she knew that she and Hex were on their own. They were wearing the only two dry suits. If they became stuck or lost in the tunnel system, there was no way anyone could come in after them.

'Good luck!' called Alex from the entrance behind them and his voice echoed faintly along the tunnel, already sounding a world away.

Amber and Hex stepped out of the end of the tunnel into a cave about four metres wide and two and a half metres high. A long gallery stretched away ahead of them into the darkness beyond their headlamp beams. As they waded towards the far end of the gallery, the ceiling began to slope downwards until they were forced to stoop as they walked. The stream deepened until they found themselves crouched at the edge of a dark pool where the roof of the cave disappeared into the water.

'Oh, dear,' said Hex. 'Dead end. We'll just collect some samples and head back.' As he unclipped a sample jar from his belt, he felt relief wash over him that he did not have to go any further. As the roof had pressed closer and closer over his bent back, Hex had been feeling the beginnings of claustrophobia.

'It's not a dead end,' said Amber. 'Where do you think the water's coming from? There's an underwater opening down there somewhere. I'll go and investigate.'

She strapped on her mask, adjusted her air flow and waded into the deepening pool. When the water was up to her neck she dived and followed the roughly ridged, sloping ceiling down until the water funnelled into a small black opening ahead. Amber held on to the ridged ceiling as she studied the opening. There was not a strong current coming from it, which was good. They would be able to swim along it fairly easily. The problem was, the opening was too narrow to turn round in and she did not know how far the tunnel went on. It could be nothing more than a water gate through to a second chamber. Or it could wind its way on into the deeper reaches of the ridge, splitting into a whole system of ever-narrowing underwater tunnels.

Hex was waiting for her at the lip of the pool as she surfaced and lifted her mask. His face was pale under the beam of his lamp. 'Dead end?' he asked hopefully.

'Nope, there's an opening. It's only small, but we should get through.'

Hex turned even paler. 'Right,' he said. Hesitantly, he waded into the pool towards her.

'I'll lead,' said Amber. 'If it goes on for too long or gets too narrow, we'll just have to back out again, OK? Remember your ice axe at your belt. You can use it to help push yourself backwards if that's what we have to do. One more thing. We should probably take the tanks off and push them ahead of us. We don't want to hook ourselves up on a rock projection or something.'

They dived down beneath the sloping ceiling and

swam down to the dark opening. Hex felt his chest squeeze painfully as he saw how small the opening was. Amber had already removed her tank and was swimming towards the hole, holding it ahead of her. Gritting his teeth, Hex slipped the tank from his shoulders and followed Amber into the tunnel.

Fifteen

Their lamps lit up the whole of the narrow space. The beams bounced off the rock walls and picked out tiny particles suspended in the water. Their air bubbles floated upwards until they became trapped against the tunnel ceiling like tiny silver balloons. Hex concentrated on breathing slow and steady as he followed Amber's kicking feet. The tunnel grew narrower and narrower, but still Amber moved on. Hex began to imagine the whole weight of the rock and earth in the ridge above him pressing down. He imagined becoming stuck and running out of air and dying in this narrow, underwater grave. He tried to turn his thoughts to something – anything – else, but they kept turning back to the tunnel and the dying and his breathing grew harsh and fast.

Suddenly Amber slowed to a stop ahead. She looked over her shoulder at him, then pointed ahead, turning on her side to let him see past her. Hex squinted along the narrow gap between Amber's body and the wall and saw that the tunnel kinked upwards. A tight band clamped itself round his chest and sweat popped out on his forehead behind the mask. Amber made an upward swooping movement with her hand, telling him that she was going to try to squeeze round the kink. Hex shook his head at her, but she had already turned away. He watched with growing horror as Amber forced her tank ahead of her. The metal cylinder scraped and clanged against the rock, then suddenly shot out of sight. Amber turned on to her back and eased herself round the kink, then she too disappeared.

Hex gazed in horror at the empty space where Amber had been. The thought of squeezing himself up into the bend was terrifying, but the alternative was to try and wriggle backwards along this wormhole that was too narrow to turn round in. He forced himself to take a few calming breaths, then pushed his own tank round the kink. Turning on to his back, he began to squirm through after Amber with his arms stretched out in front of him. For one dreadful moment he was stuck in the bend, unable to move, then his groping hands were gripped by another hand and Amber pulled him through.

Hex gasped with relief behind his mask as his head broke the surface. They were in a long, shallow opening with a ceiling just centimetres above his head, but at least he could spread his arms out to the side without meeting rock. They swam along the narrow passage for ninety metres until the shallow air pocket widened into a large chamber with a banking clay floor.

Hex and Amber crawled out of the water on to the bank, dragging their tanks behind them. They sat on the cold clay in the darkness and took off their masks, then turned their heads back and forth, letting their lamps pick out the details of the vast chamber. It was about twelve metres high, and all around, from ceiling to floor, great frozen waterfalls of white calcite hung from the chamber walls. Pillars of rock supported the high ceiling and an underwater stream wound its way through the chamber, disappearing into the tunnel they had just emerged from.

Hex had never felt so glad to have so much space above his head.

'Are you OK?' asked Amber, watching him critically.

'I'm not enjoying this at all,' admitted Hex.

'But you loved diving in Hudson Bay,' said Amber.

'This is different. It's so . . . closed in.' Hex shuddered. 'I think I'm a bit claustrophobic,' he admitted, wiping the sweat from his forehead.

'Not a good time to find out,' said Amber. 'Do you want to stay here and wait for me?'

'No,' said Hex determinedly. 'Dive-buddy system, remember? We stay together.'

They strapped on their tanks and walked to the other end of the chamber where, again, the ceiling sloped downwards into another pool. 'It looks like a system of gentle overflows,' said Amber. 'The stream runs from one chamber to the next, all the way down through the ridge. They must connect up to the old mine workings at some point. That's how the cyanide gets through into the river. If we keep going, we should find a way into the mine. Ready?'

Hex nodded reluctantly and they dived again. This time the tunnel Amber led them into was wider, but long, pointed stalactites thrust down from the roof like the teeth of some huge monster and they had to weave their way through them, taking care not to tear their suits against the rough edges. A torn suit meant death from hypothermia in water this cold.

They came out into a circular chamber where water dripped constantly from the stalactites that hung from the low roof. Amber and Hex trod water and turned slowly so that the beams of the lamps strapped to their heads lit up the walls of the chamber. The rock rose from the water, sheer and unbroken on all sides. They had reached a dead end.

Hex wrenched off his mask and threw his head back, taking deep gasps of air. It was cold and damp, with a slightly metallic taste, but anything was better than having to suck air into his lungs through the confines of his mask. His feelings of claustrophobia were growing worse by the second and he was close to panic at the thought of diving back into the dark water and forcing his way through the forest of stalactites for a second time.

'Hex?' asked Amber, pushing off her mask and giving him a worried look.

Hex realized he was still gasping with his head flung back. With a great effort, he made himself relax and breathe more slowly. 'I can't believe you do this for fun,' he said, with only a slight quaver to his voice.

Amber studied his pale face in her headlamp beam. 'You know we have to double back, right?'

Hex nodded. He did not trust himself to speak again.

'You're doing fine, Hex,' said Amber, without a hint of her usual sarcasm. 'You just let me know when you're ready, OK?'

'Now,' said Hex promptly. 'Let's go now.' He was frightened that if he waited any longer, he would lose his nerve.

'Two things,' said Amber. 'You need to coil in your safety line as you double back. If you leave loose rope around, you're in much more danger of getting hooked up on something.'

'No loose line. Right,' said Hex. 'And the other thing?'

'Visibility might not be so good second time round,' said Amber reluctantly.

'What? How? It can't get any darker. This whole place is as black as Hell.'

'There was a thick layer of silt on the bottom of the tunnel,' explained Amber. 'And we're bound to have disturbed some of it as we came through the first time.'

'Oh, that's just great,' said Hex and his voice echoed hollowly around the cavern. 'We have to swim back through silt soup.'

'Just follow your line and stay calm,' said Amber.

As Hex swam towards the stalactite tunnel, he could see a cloud of suspended silt particles pouring out of the entrance like smoke from a chimney. With growing dread, he watched Amber disappear into the murky water. He had an irrational urge to return to the surface of the circular chamber and stay there until his air ran out, but he forced himself into the tunnel after Amber.

Almost immediately, visibility was reduced to nearly zero. His lamp beam could not penetrate the whirling silt particles. They acted like a wall, reflecting the light back at him. Just ahead of him, Amber was moving as smoothly as she could, but more silt was puffing up from the floor of the tunnel all the time. Hex felt as though he was crawling as slowly as a snail as he inched forward with one hand following his line and the other hand outstretched in front of him, but all too soon he was into the stalactite forest.

Using his hands to guide him round the rough-edged stalactites, Hex squeezed himself through the gaps. The clanging of his tank against the stone rang like hammer blows and he was finding it harder and harder to suck enough air into his lungs. Finally, convinced that his tank must be nearly empty, he stopped and checked his gauge in the dim circle of his lamp beam. There was plenty of air left in the tank. Hex felt relief flood through him and his breathing immediately became easier. He prepared to move on again, and realized he did not know which way to swim.

He had been taking up the slack on his safety line as Amber had told him, but he had dropped the coils of rope in his panic to check the gauge and now his line hung straight down from his waist. Was he pointing in the direction Amber had gone or was he facing back towards the circular chamber? Had he turned in the water as he checked his gauge? Hex decided he hadn't and pushed himself forward. He squeezed past one side of a jagged stalactite, then changed his mind and turned back, edging round the other side to his original position.

Hex emerged from the gap, then stopped and peered through the cloudy water at a stalactite less than a metre in front of him. It had a teardrop-shaped hole through its centre. Suddenly he was sure he had just passed that stalactite. He turned again and squeezed back into the narrow space between the jagged stalactite and the tunnel wall. He was halfway through when he came to a sudden halt.

Hex grabbed the rock projections on each side of him more firmly and pulled harder. He managed to squeeze forward a few centimetres before his safety line tightened around his waist. With a thrill of horror, he realized that he had forgotten to take in the slack before he moved off again. The line had become wrapped round the jagged stalactite and was anchoring him in place.

Stay calm, thought Hex. Just back up and free the rope.

He began to push himself backwards but was jerked to a halt as one of his tank straps caught on a spar of rock. Now he was truly stuck, wedged into the narrow gap between the wall and the jagged stalactite, unable to move forward because of the safety line and unable to move back because of the snagged tank strap.

Hex tried to draw his arms back into the gap in order to unfasten the harness that held his tank to his back. His elbows were too big to squeeze down into the space between his ribs and the rock. All of a sudden, the panic came flooding in. His chest and throat contracted and he could not breathe. The ability to think rationally deserted him and, desperate for more air, he ripped his mask off and let it drop. A flurry of bubbles burst past his face and he closed his eyes as he realized what he had just done. Now his mask was trailing in the water, somewhere below his chest, and there was no way he could reach it with his arms stuck out in front of him.

Hex struggled until his lungs were bursting, but he remained wedged between the stalactite and the tunnel wall. His face twisted as he slumped against the rock and tried to hold his breath for a few seconds more. His worst nightmare was about to come true. He was going to die, alone and trapped, in the dark confines of an underwater tunnel.

SIXTEEN

A circle of pale light appeared in front of him and Hex felt a glimmer of hope. Either he was hallucinating, or Amber was making her way back to him. He focused on the light, willing Amber to reach him in time. The blood was roaring in his ears and bright spots of light were dancing behind his eyes. He had seconds left before his aching lungs gave up the battle to hold on to his last breath of air.

The light grew stronger, then suddenly he could see Amber's face through the swirling silt. She reached out and grabbed his hands as his lungs finally gave up and the breath exploded from his mouth in huge, silvery bubbles. An instant later she had detached the mouthpiece from her mask and pushed it into his mouth. Gratefully, Hex sucked on it, pulling air into his lungs again and again.

Amber reached down, retrieved his own mask and mouthpiece and brought them up to his face. For a few seconds Hex would not let go of Amber's mouthpiece, but then he reluctantly allowed her to make the exchange, grabbing at his own mouthpiece with the strength of panic.

Minutes passed as Amber worked first to free his safety line, then to unhook his tank harness. Hex sucked in air and concentrated on staying calm. Finally, he could move again. Amber held his arms as he eased away from the stalactite that had nearly killed him. Once he was out, he gave her hands a squeeze of thanks, then he took up the slack on his safety line and they moved off through the dark water together, weaving through the stalactites until they emerged once again into the pool at the end of the high-roofed chamber they had started from.

'I have never been so scared in my life,' groaned

Hex as he waded to the edge of the pool. He stood knee-deep in the freezing water and waited for his panicked breathing to slow back to normal. 'I am never, ever doing this again. I nearly died.' He looked at Amber. 'Thanks,' he said simply.

'No problem,' said Amber, grinning at him. 'Give me a minute. I'll see if I can find the right tunnel this time.'

As Hex waited for Amber to emerge from the pool, he dried off and reassembled his mask and mouthpiece. He fussed with the equipment for a lot longer than was necessary, to stop himself from thinking about what he had to do next. Even if he gave up now and turned back, he would still have to make his way through the wormhole with the kink at the end. Hex shuddered. He did not know whether he could do this.

'Found it!' yelled Amber, emerging from the pool and ripping off her mask. 'We're nearly there, Hex!'

Before he could think about it too much, Hex put on his mask and dived into the pool after Amber. This time, she led him to a long, narrow horizontal crack splitting the rock wall. Hex felt a surge of hope. This looked like the sort of fault that might be caused by mining. Amber could be right. They could be about to reach their destination.

They squeezed through the crack and emerged into a flooded shaft. The floor was littered with rotting timbers, rusting buckets and other mining debris. They swam up until they broke surface, then trod water as they looked around. The shaft rose up above them, climbing to a rock ceiling as high as a cathedral. Over to one side of the shaft, a floodlit metal platform was suspended above the water and a metal staircase zigzagged up the shaft wall to a floodlit tunnel three quarters of the way up. Thick lengths of industrial hosing hung like spaghetti from the high tunnel, ending just above the water.

'We've got him,' whispered Hex, pointing to the dirty brown liquid dripping from the pipes into the clear water at the bottom of the shaft.

They climbed out on to the metal platform and, while Hex filmed the incriminating scene, Amber leaned as far as she could over the edge of the platform to hold a sample jar under the dripping hoses.

Suddenly, a motor started up in the tunnel above the shaft and the pipes began to quiver. Then the top of the pipes bulged as cyanide waste was pumped into them. Amber yanked her arm away and fell back on to the platform as gallons of dirty brown liquid spurted out of the bottom of the pipes. The air filled with the bitter odour of almonds as the pipes swayed crazily back and forth, spraying the waste all around the bottom of the shaft.

Amber and Hex had removed their masks and air hoses while they collected their evidence, but now the air was filled with a fine mist of cyanide solution. 'Mask!' yelled Hex, above the roar of the pressurized liquid and the clattering of the swinging pipes. He grabbed Amber and dragged her with him into the furthest corner of the platform. 'Put your mask on!'

They huddled in the corner, using their tanks to breathe while the waste cyanide poured down around them. Hex filmed the outpouring from the pipes for five long minutes until, finally, the flow began to slow down. Up in the tunnel at the top of the shaft, the note of the pump engine changed as the reservoir of waste it was tapping drained away. Then the pump engine was turned off and the pipes slowly settled back against the wall again. Amber and Hex clambered to their feet and walked to the edge of the platform, pushing their masks off their faces. The water below them was now a foaming, brown soup.

Hex felt his stomach churn. It had been a nightmare journey through the silt-filled tunnel. Could he do it again? Even as his mind told him there was no other way out, he could not help looking hopefully up at the metal stairway with the dry, bright tunnel waiting at the top of it. As he looked up, his heart clenched with shock. A man was standing at the end of the tunnel looking down at him.

For an instant they stared at one another, both equally shocked. Then the man ducked back into the tunnel and Hex could hear his shouts of alarm echoing down the shaft. 'Come on,' he said, stepping on to the edge of the platform and turning back to Amber. 'Time to disappear.'

Amber stared at him wide-eyed, but made no move to join him. 'I can't,' she said.

'Don't be stupid!' snapped Hex. 'If I can do it a second time, why can't you!'

For answer, Amber held out her arm. Her dry suit was ripped open from elbow to wrist.

'I caught it on the edge of the platform, when I pulled back from the pipes,' she said in a trembling voice.

Hex stared at the ripped dry suit in horror. There was no way Amber could go back into the cyanide-laced water now. If she didn't die of hypothermia first, the poison would get into her system. Either way she would be killed.

'All right,' said Hex, desperately looking about him. 'All right. We'll try to get out another way.'

'No,' said Amber, her voice firming up as she realized how it had to be. 'I'll try to get out another way. You're going back through the caves. You've got the safety rope to guide you all the way back to the others.'

'I'm not leaving you,' said Hex, shaking his head.

'This is no time to play the hero!' snapped Amber. 'You have to get out!' She reached out and touched the camcorder strung around his neck. 'This is my only chance, Hex. We already know Usher is prepared to kill us. If we both stay here, he gets the evidence – and we're dead. You have to get out and take this to the authorities. Get them here as soon as you can, Hex. It's my only chance.'

Hex's shoulders slumped as he realized Amber was right. Claustrophobia or not, he had to make the journey back through the tunnels – alone – or all their efforts would have been wasted and Papaluk would have died in vain. And there was no time to simply swap suits.

Amber untied her safety line and handed it to Hex, then she reached up on tiptoe and gave him a quick kiss on the cheek. 'See you later,' she whispered.

Hex groaned, then pulled down his mask, turned and jumped into the shaft.

Left alone on the platform, Amber ripped off her tank and weight belt and threw them into the flooded shaft. Then she turned and sprinted up the metal staircase in a desperate attempt to get to the top before the security guards appeared and cut off her escape.

'They must've reached the mine,' said Li, as the line in her hand stopped unravelling. 'Amber's not moving.'

'Yes, Hex too has stopped,' confirmed Paulo.

Alex had been sitting on a snow-covered rock on the river bank, resting his shoulder, but he stood up and came to join Li and Paulo. 'Do you think they're OK?' he asked, peering down into the water.

'Amber's an expert diver,' said Li. 'They'll be fine. You watch, they'll be back out any time now—'

She stuttered to a halt as the water flowing out of the hole in the rock face suddenly turned brown and increased in volume until it was filling the opening. 'Oh, no!' cried Li, catching the odour of bitter almonds rising from the water. 'They're dumping cyanide! What can we do?'

Paulo shook his head grimly as he stared down at the water. 'We can only wait. They will get out when they can. Their dry suits will protect them.'

Five anxious minutes later, Li felt a tugging on the safety line she held. 'Amber's on the move!' she yelled.

'And Hex,' said Paulo. 'Shall I start to pull in the rope?'

'No,' said Alex. 'As long as they're moving, let them swim at their own pace. Just reel it in enough to keep the line straight, so they've got something to guide them. I don't think they can see much in this water.'

'Here they are!' cried Li as she heard someone wading along the tunnel towards them. But only Hex burst out of the opening in the rock. He was clutching Amber's safety rope in his hand and his eyes were wild behind his mask.

'Top of the ridge,' he panted as he ripped his mask and safety line off and dumped his tank. 'We have to get to the top of the ridge! Amber's trying to find another way out.'

They followed Hex as he sprinted off without waiting to explain.

By the time the others caught up with him he was lying full length at the top of the ridge. His breath was tearing in and out of his throat with ragged gasps and his gaze raked back and forth across the complex below.

'Her suit tore,' he gasped. 'She was going to try to find another way out through the mine—'

Hex stopped and the hope faded from his eyes as he focused on a group of five figures emerging from behind the carbon processing huts. Four of the figures were security guards. The fifth figure was slumped between two of the guards, with her head down and her feet dragging through the snow. It was Amber.

Hex cursed and slammed his fist into the snow. The guards dragged Amber over to a low, windowless building situated next to the helicopter pad. As they approached the building, the door opened and a man who they recognized as Daniel Usher stepped out. The two guards with Amber's arms draped around their shoulders half-carried, half-dragged her up the steps and into the building. Daniel Usher barked instructions to the other two guards and they ran off, speaking into their radios.

Usher lifted his head and stared around the perimeter of the mine workings. He seemed to look straight at Alpha Force as they lay at the top of the ridge and they all ducked, even though they knew they were hidden from sight under the trees.

There were security guards running everywhere on the site. An alarm was sounding and vehicles were roaring off to the perimeter fences. As Daniel Usher went back into the building and closed the door, the company helicopter's rotors began to turn.

'We have to hide,' said Alex, as the helicopter rose into the air and began quartering the site. 'Come on! The tree cover's too thin up here. We can't help Amber if we get caught too.'

They raced down the slope and into the thicker trees below, just as the helicopter flew low overhead. Alex was wincing with pain as his injured shoulder jogged up and down, but he ran as fast as the rest of them. Alex, Hex and Paulo squeezed on to the little sled while Li grabbed one of Amber's mittens and took it around to Ice. 'Come on, boy!' she said, holding the mitten under his nose. 'For Amber!'

Ice rose to his feet and snarled at the other dogs to get them up. Li hurried round to the back of the sled and climbed on. The team was one dog short and, with three passengers, the sled was overloaded, but as soon as Li released the brake, Ice leaned into his harness with all his strength. 'Hike!' called Li. The other dogs took up the strain and, as the helicopter passed overhead for another sweep, the dogs took off, pulling the sled deeper into the woods below the ridge.

SEVENTEEN

Amber frowned as she came to. Her head hurt. She lifted her hand and gently probed her scalp, just above her ear. There was a tender lump there.

'How did that happen?' she wondered aloud, and as she said it, she instantly remembered everything. She remembered the headlong dash up the metal steps and the frantic scrabbling to get into the tiny space between the pump generator and the tunnel wall. Once there, she had crouched, motionless, as security guards ran back and forth searching for her. She had waited until enough time had passed for

Hex to make it safely out of the tunnels, then she had made her own break for freedom. It had been a doomed attempt. Instantly, four security guards had spotted her. She remembered fighting hard in their grip until one of them had cracked her across the side of the head. The thick, vulcanized rubber of her dry suit had absorbed most of the blow, but it had still been enough to send her crashing to the concrete floor. She remembered trying to get up again, but then a red mist had come down over her eyes and she had passed out.

So, where was she now? And was she alone?

Amber listened. She could hear the gentle hum of a heating system and, faintly, the rise and fall of classical music. She opened her eyes just a crack and peered out under her lashes. She was lying in bed, in a luxurious bedroom, and she seemed to be alone. Opening her eyes, she sat up. The cream silk sheet that had been covering her slipped down and Amber realized that she was naked. She snatched up the sheet and held it up to her chin as her reeling brain tried to get a grasp on the situation. She had passed out in a cold concrete tunnel in a gold mine in northern

Canada. She had woken up in a bedroom that would not be out of place in Hollywood's Hotel Bel-Air. Except that there were no windows.

She looked around for something – anything – to wear and saw a dinner dress laid out at the bottom of the bed.

'Just call me Bond. Amber Bond,' she muttered, hooking the dress towards her. It was a designer dress, made of a soft, white material, and it was exactly the right size. Amber slipped it on and swung her legs out over the edge of the bed. Her feet sank into the thick carpet as she made her way to the bedroom door.

As the door swung open, the classical music grew louder. Amber stepped out into the corridor and walked towards another door, which was slightly ajar. She could hear the clink of silver cutlery on bone china. Amber eased up to the door and peered through the gap on the hinge side of the frame.

'Come in, Amber,' said a familiar voice.

Daniel Usher! She felt a huge rage sweep through her as she realized that the man who had paid to have her parents killed was on the other side of the door. She wanted to rush into the room, put her hands around his neck and squeeze until he stopped breathing. With a great effort, she brought herself under control. This situation needed very careful handling.

Amber drew herself up to her full height and stepped through the door. She walked into another softly lit, windowless room. Daniel Usher was sitting at the head of a long dining table, surrounded by plates of beautifully prepared food.

'How good to meet you again, Amber,' he said.

'Aren't you supposed to be stroking a Persian cat or something?' said Amber.

'Excuse me?'

'You know. "Come in, Mr Bond. I have been waiting for you,"' said Amber.

Daniel Usher laughed softly. 'Ah! I see. I am the villain. I haven't seen you since, oh . . .'

'Since you had my parents killed,' said Amber flatly.

'You have been busy,' said Usher, without missing a beat. 'It must be three years since then. You've grown. The dress fits you well. It belongs to my daughter. She left it the last time she was here.'

'Where's here?' demanded Amber.

'Oh, we're still at the mine.' He smiled. 'All that snow and ugliness is right outside the door of my little hideaway.' Amber suddenly remembered the windowless building next to the helicopter pad that she had seen from the top of the ridge.

Usher lifted the lid from a serving dish and helped himself to a pork chop. As the rich smell of the grilled meat drifted over to her, Amber felt a stab of pain in her abdomen. Her legs went weak and she staggered slightly. She frowned and focused on the jug of iced water, suddenly realizing how terribly thirsty she was.

'How long have I been . . .'

'Unconscious? Not long. Fifteen minutes or so. Don't worry, you don't have a cracked skull. It was more of a faint, really. Are you sure you're quite well, Amber?'

Amber tore her gaze away from the water and glared at him, trying to ignore the way her eyes kept blurring.

'I had the site nurse brought in to check you over,' he continued. 'It was she who undressed you, by the way, in case you were wondering. She found this around your waist.' He held up Amber's belt pouch, containing her insulin pens and blood sugar testing kit. 'I wonder, Amber . . . How long is it since you had a dose of insulin?'

Daniel Usher stared at Amber and she felt a cold chill run through her. Her last dose had been early in the morning, before breakfast. Even on a normal day, she would be due another dose by now, and the emotional stress of the last few hours must have really pushed up her blood sugar levels. Usher was right. The blow to the head was not the reason she had passed out. The abdominal pain, acute thirst and muscle weakness she was experiencing now were all early signs of dangerously high blood sugar levels, or hyperglycaemia. If she did not get insulin soon, the symptoms would worsen. The abdominal pains would become more severe and she would start vomiting. Her breathing would become laboured as she became more dehydrated and then she would fall into a coma.

Amber shrugged. 'I'm fine,' she said, sauntering over to the water jug and pouring herself a glass. She must not show him how important that little belt pouch full of insulin was to her. As she poured, her vision blurred again and the water slopped over on to the table.

'Oops,' he said. 'Looks like those nasty old blood sugar levels are rising.'

'I said, I'm fine,' grated Amber. She lifted the glass to her lips and tried not to drink too fast.

'If you say so.' Usher slipped the little pouch into the inside pocket of his beautifully cut suit jacket and frowned at the bulge it made. 'Hmm, best not,' he said, removing the pouch and laying it on the table. 'I need to look good for my broadcast tonight. I'm announcing my intention to run for governor. In fact, I must be leaving for the airport quite soon if I'm to get to the television studios in time. So, let's get down to business, shall we? Please sit.'

Amber wanted to refuse, but her legs were in danger of collapsing under her. She pulled out a chair and sat at the table, giving him a cool stare. It was time to make her move.

'You might as well not bother with your broadcast. You won't be running for office because you'll be on trial for murder. We have evidence that you arranged to have Papaluk killed because she found out about you dumping cyanide into the river.'

'Yes, what a pity you and your four friends became . . . involved in that,' he sighed. 'Killing the Eskimo would have been such a neat, simple solution.'

'Inuit,' snapped Amber. 'Papaluk was an Inuit.'

'And what became of my colleague?'

'You mean your hired killer?'

Daniel Usher sighed as though he was finding this whole business a tedious nuisance. 'I'm presuming he is dead . . .'

'Yes, he is,' said Amber.

'So, it was you and your friends who sent me his final text message?'

'Yes.'

'Very good, Amber! I must admit it fooled me for a while. But I'm way ahead of you now.'

He picked up his mobile phone and flicked it open.

'What are you going to do?' asked Amber.

'I'm going to have a little chat with your friends.'

'You don't have a contact number.'

'Ah, now that's where you're wrong,' smiled Daniel Usher.

Eighteen

Hex was hunched over his palmtop in the middle of the forest, still dressed in his dry suit.

Li, Alex and Paulo were watching the screen over his shoulder. Hex had already downloaded the images from his camcorder into the palmtop and now he was waiting to connect to the Net so that he could send the evidence to the police.

'Come on! Come on!' he muttered, glaring at the screen of his palmtop. The flat aerial in the lid had not yet connected to the communications satellite and the time was ticking by. It was twenty-five minutes since Amber had been captured and for every one of those twenty-five minutes, Hex had bitterly regretted leaving her behind in the mine. He could not get it out of his head that virtually the last words he had said to her were, 'Don't be so stupid.'

'Yes!' he hissed as the palmtop finally made the connection. 'We're through.' He flexed his fingers, held them poised above the keyboard – and stopped. A mobile phone was ringing. It was coming from his jacket, which was bundled up on the sled behind him. Someone was calling Daniel Usher's hired killer.

Hex looked at the others, then reached back and pulled the phone from his jacket. He flipped it open, put it to his ear and listened. His face twisted with anger. 'Usher!' he snapped. 'If you've hurt her—'

Hex stopped and listened some more. 'Yes. I understand.'

He switched off the phone, then reached out to his palmtop and changed the destination address of the downloaded information. 'I'm sending a copy of this to a hacker friend of mine. He'll store it for me, in case something happens to us.'

'What about contacting the police?' asked Paulo.

'Change of plan,' said Hex, severing the connection to the Net. He looked up at the others and his green eyes were full of a cold anger. 'That was Daniel Usher. He's holding Amber hostage. He's taken her insulin away from her. He reckons she's got a couple of hours left before she falls into a coma. If we bring the camcorder tape to the mine, with the camcorder, he'll give her back her insulin. If not, she dies. Luckily, he doesn't seem to know about my palmtop, but he warned me that he has men monitoring police frequencies and news sites. If there is any hint of a leak about this before we get there, Amber dies.'

Alex swore softly. 'So he wants us to just walk in there?'

'He knows there are four of us. He wants us all. He says they'll be expecting us at the main gate.'

'I bet they will,' muttered Alex.

'If we do walk in, do you think he'll keep his side of the bargain?' asked Li.

'Hell, no,' said Hex grimly. 'Total containment. That's what he's after.'

'But we can't leave Amber to die!' cried Li.

'Of course not,' said Hex, packing away his palmtop.

'So what do we do?'

'We go in there and get her out,' said Hex.

While Hex changed out of his dry suit, the others dumped all the baggage except for the medical kit and Amber's arctic clothes and boots, which eased the load for the dogs and made just enough room for three passengers on the sled. Paulo took Amber's spare insulin pens from the medical kit and carefully stored them in the inside pocket of his jacket before joining Hex and Alex on the sled. Li grabbed one of Amber's mittens and walked to the front of the team. She squatted down in front of Ice, who regarded her with his blue eyes full of haughty disdain. Li held out the mitten to the dog. He sniffed it, then let out a whine.

'We're going to go find her, Ice,' said Li. 'We're going to find Amber!' The dog's ears perked up at the name and he rose to his feet. Li hurried to her place on the back of the sled, released the brake and cried, 'Let's go!'

Ice took off like a bullet and the other dogs picked up his excitement. They ran smoothly and the sled raced through the trees, heading away from the river and towards the quarry end of the mine in a long, shallow curve.

An hour later, Alpha Force was in position on the quarry side of the mine. They had left the dogs in the woods behind the quarry, still harnessed to the sled in case they needed a fast getaway. The sled brake was rammed down hard into the snow, and for extra anchorage they had attached a snow-hook to the gangline and embedded it in the ground.

A few metres away from where they were lying, the perimeter fence of the mine stretched across the snowy ground. Beyond the fence was the open pit of the quarry, cratered and pitted like the surface of the moon.

Hex glanced at his watch, then looked impatiently at the setting sun. Time was short, but they had to wait until dark before they moved in. Beyond the quarry, armed security guards were patrolling the main gate area and the perimeter fence below the ridge, but the quarry itself was deserted, apart from the quarry workers.

Alex peered down at the workers. The slab of rock that had been blasted away from the quarry side in the earlier explosion had now all been broken up and hauled over to the leach pads in the big-wheeled trucks. The quarrymen were busy preparing another explosive charge and Alpha Force had deliberately positioned themselves close to the section of quarry wall that was to be blasted.

'This might just work,' muttered Alex, watching the progress of the blasting work. The sun was dipping below the horizon. In a few minutes it would be dark.

Below them, the generator that powered the floodlights started up with a clatter, then built up to a steady whine. All around the site, the floodlights came on, lighting up every dark corner and giving each security guard a four-pointed shadow.

'Something's happening,' whispered Li, pointing to the helicopter pad. The pilot of Daniel Usher's private helicopter had clambered into his seat and was starting up the machine. As the rotor blades began to turn, Usher emerged from the windowless building with a fur-trimmed parka over his suit jacket and his trousers tucked into fur-lined boots.

'He's getting out before the dirty business starts,' said Li, watching as Usher climbed up into the helicopter.

'It's his broadcast tonight,' said Hex, remembering what he had read on the Net. 'He's heading for the airport, then on to his company's nearest television studio.'

The helicopter took off and banked away over the trees as the sun disappeared below the horizon. In the quarry, the men waited for the helicopter to move well out of the air space above the mine, then they returned to their preparations with a new sense of purpose.

Alex looked up at the darkening sky, then down at the quarry. 'Is everyone clear about what they have to do?'

The others nodded.

Alex looked down at the quarry again. Someone was hoisting the red flag. 'Showtime,' he said.

Nineteen

They each pulled their goggles down over their eyes and laced their hoods tightly around the goggles so that their noses and mouths were covered. Paulo and Li wormed forward through the snow to the fence. As soon as they had cut a hole in the mesh, Alex and Hex came up to join them, with Alex squirming along on his side in an attempt to protect his injured shoulder.

The klaxon went off with a howl that echoed around the quarry, and all the workers retreated to a safe distance. Alpha Force squirmed through the hole in the fence and crouched in the darkness, waiting for the explosion. When it came, it was deafening. As the detonators went off, a huge slab of rock lifted out of the wall just over to their left, then crashed down to the quarry floor. The ground under their feet shook violently and the shock waves from the blast buffeted them. Then they were on their feet and running as the thick dust cloud they had been waiting for filled the quarry.

Lumps of stone and dirt rained down on them. The dust was thick and choking, swirling in the air, but they had all memorized their route as they lay hidden in the trees and knew exactly where they were going. Their eyes and noses were protected from the worst of it, but still the thick dust coated their goggles and clogged their throats and noses in a gritty layer. Alpha Force kept running. They all had to be in position by the time the dust cleared and already they could see the milky glow of floodlights through the haze.

As they reached the edge of the quarry, Alpha Force split up, each running for a different target. They were now coming out of the thickest part of the dust cloud, and for a few seconds they would be in the glare of the floodlights and in great danger of being spotted.

Alex ran for the guardhouse next to the main gate, keeping his head down and clutching his injured arm to his chest. Every time he jumped or swerved to avoid a lump of rock, the pain twisted in his shoulder like broken glass, but he gritted his teeth and kept on running. He had insisted on being part of the rescue mission, so now he could not let Amber down.

Hex and Li swerved off to the left, running for the shelter of a fleet of trucks parked next to the leach pads. Li could feel her heart beating in her ears. Every second she was expecting a shot to ring out, but the armed guards were concentrating on the land beyond the perimeter fence and she managed to reach the first truck without being spotted. She slid under the truck to safety, and a split second later, Hex flung himself down beside her. They shared an incredulous look through dust-smeared goggles. They had made it! Then they both closed their eyes tight and waited for Paulo to do his bit.

At the same time, Alex reached the back of the

guardhouse by the main gate. Like most buildings in this part of Canada, it was built on short stilts to insulate it from the frozen ground. Alex eased himself underneath the building and lay there with his nose centimetres from the raised floor, trying to slow his breathing. Two guards were standing at the front of the building next to the gate and he did not want them to hear him. It was dark under the guardhouse, but still Alex raised his good hand and covered his eyes. It was all up to Paulo now.

Paulo had had the shortest distance to run. While the other three were still racing for their hiding places, he was already in position. He was crouched on a concrete platform in the shadow of the big generator that was powering the floodlights. Peering under the vibrating generator, he located the fuel pipe and gripped it in his gloved hand. Shutting his eyes tightly, he counted to twenty then tensed his muscles and ripped the fuel pipe out of the generator with one hard yank.

The big machine sputtered, caught, sputtered again, then chugged to a stop. An instant later, all around the complex, the floodlights winked out.

Shouts erupted from all sides. Paulo and Hex both scrambled out of their separate hiding places and started running towards the windowless building where Amber was being held. For a short time, they had an advantage over the armed guards in the complex. They had their night vision.

Li crept out from under her truck and began working her way along the line of vehicles, easing open the cab doors and pulling the keys from the ignition. She worked as quickly and quietly as she could but she did not have much time. Already, torches were being turned on and their beams bobbed and dipped in the hands of running guards.

Alex waited under the guardhouse. The guards inside had turned out the lights and then stumbled from the building, not wanting to be a well-lit target. Alex waited until he was sure the guards had all gone, then he crawled out and slipped up the steps into the building. Once inside, he quickly found what he was looking for. The green and red buttons on the panel that controlled the main gate were glowing softly in the darkness. Alex pressed the green button, and outside, unnoticed, the big double gates swung silently open. Alex was heading out to join Hex and Paulo when a torch beam skittered past the guardhouse window.

Alex dropped to the floor and crouched there, listening for any movement outside. He gave it five seconds before deciding that the torch beam had been a random event and the coast was clear. He was about to stand again when a waste bin under the desk caught his eye. Alex frowned. Something familiar was sticking up out of the bin. Reaching inside, he pulled out Amber's insulin pouch. His face tightened with anger as he opened the pouch and saw broken insulin pens inside. This was final proof, if he had needed it, that Daniel Usher had never planned on keeping his word. Total containment. Those were the instructions he had left with his guards.

Paulo and Hex had reached the windowless building without being spotted. Hex tried the door and was surprised to find it unlocked. They flattened themselves against the wall on either side of the door and Hex pushed it open. Silence. Hex stuck his head round the door. He saw an empty, carpeted corridor, with several closed doors leading off it. Quietly they slipped inside and the door sighed shut behind them. It was warm and quiet here. They pulled off their goggles and flung back their hoods.

'Amber!' called Hex softly.

There was no reply.

Paulo and Hex shared a look, then Hex pointed at the first door and Paulo nodded. Together they moved silently towards it.

In the vehicle compound, Li jumped from the step of the last truck in the row and eased the door shut. She had a dozen sets of ignition keys clutched in her hands. She looked around for a place to dump them and spotted the first of the leach pads a few metres away. She hurried over and threw the keys into the murky brown liquid. They splashed into the cyanide solution and sank amongst the crushed rocks below the surface. Li nodded in satisfaction then gasped as an arm came over her shoulder and locked around her throat.

She simultaneously rammed her elbows back into her attacker's solar plexus and stamped her foot down on the inside of his ankle bone. While he was still reeling in pain, she tried to twist out of the crook of his arm. She nearly made it, but at the last second the guard caught hold of her hood. She let out a cry as it was yanked back, along with a handful of her long, black hair. She spun to face him and her hair fanned out around her.

The guard gaped. 'You're a girl!'

'And you're an idiot,' snapped Li, kicking the gun from his hand.

The guard lunged, arms outstretched. Li turned sideways, grabbed one of his arms and braced her leg. One heave and the guard soared over her shoulder into the cyanide pond. He surfaced, coughing and spluttering. A smell of bitter almonds filled the air as he threshed in the brown liquid. Li turned to run but the man began to choke in the fumes from the liquid. He stopped struggling to reach the edge of the pond and went under. Li hesitated, then grabbed a long hooked pole lying by the pond. The next time the man surfaced, she hooked the back of his jacket and hauled him up on to the edge of the pond. She nodded. Now he had a chance. She left him slumped there, picked up his pistol, dropped the pole and ran.

Li and Alex arrived at the windowless building together, eased open the door and disappeared inside. All the doors leading off the carpeted corridor were open, but there was no sign of Paulo and Hex.

Alex pressed his good hand against the wall and leaned over, retching. His face was drawn with pain.

'Are you OK?' hissed Li. 'You don't look so good.'

'Have you seen yourself lately?' whispered Alex, grinning despite himself. Li was covered from head to foot in quarry dust, except for two white circles around her eyes where her goggles had been. With her tangled hair sticking up all over the place, she looked like a startled koala.

Alex straightened up and headed down the corridor. 'Paulo? Hex? Have you found her?' he hissed, checking each doorway in turn. 'We have to move it. We've been lucky so far but those guards are starting to get themselves organized out there.'

'Where are they?' whispered Li, then jumped as two dark shapes emerged from the end doorway. It was Hex and Paulo and their faces were grim.

'What's the matter?' asked Li.

'We've searched everywhere,' said Hex. 'The building's empty.'

'What!' gasped Alex.

'She is not here,' said Paulo. 'Amber is not here.'

Twenty

'Well, Amber. It's been delightful, but I have to leave now.'

Amber lifted her head from the table and stared blearily at the man standing over her. 'OK,' she mumbled, grimacing at the pains in her abdomen. Her tongue felt too big for her mouth and her throat was as dry as ashes.

The man flicked open his mobile phone. 'Prepare the 'copter and send Harris over here,' he ordered.

Amber licked her lips and tried to focus on the table in front of her. She needed a drink desperately and she had a vague memory of a jug full of iced water. She spotted the jug and, with a great effort of concentration, managed to grab the handle and pull it towards her. It was empty. Amber could have sobbed with disappointment. Why was she so thirsty?

A faint warning bell began to ring at the back of her mind. She was thirsty because she needed . . . 'Insulin.'

For a few seconds Amber puzzled over this strange word that had popped out of her mouth, trying to figure out what it meant. Then she focused on her insulin pouch, lying on the table by the man's perfectly manicured hand. With a jolt, her mind cleared and she remembered what was happening to her. Daniel Usher was holding her hostage. He had taken her insulin away from her, and unless she did something soon, she was going to die.

Daniel Usher got up, walked away from the table and picked up a fur-trimmed parka. As his back was turned, Amber stretched out her arm and grasped the pouch. There was a knock on the outer door and Daniel Usher went to open it. Amber pulled the pouch towards her and grasped the zip tab. Her fingers felt huge and boneless, but on the third try she managed to pull the zip open.

She stared stupidly at the things inside the pouch for a few seconds, then reached in and grabbed hold of the insulin pen with her balloon fingers. The pouch dropped to the floor, but that didn't matter. She had her insulin pen and she wasn't going to die after all. She pulled the white dinner dress up and positioned the pen on the fleshy part of her thigh.

'Good try, Amber,' said Daniel Usher, grasping her hand and pulling the pen from her fingers. Amber watched helplessly as he snapped the insulin pen in half, dropped it into the pouch and handed it to the guard who had come into the room after him. 'Dispose of this when you leave, will you, Harris?'

'Yes, sir. And when the other four turn up?'

'Dispose of them too.'

'And this one?'

'She's disposing of herself, aren't you, Amber? When she's dead, leave all the bodies together, somewhere well away from the mine. Somewhere where they won't be found until the spring thaw. Tragic accident and all that.'

'Yes, sir. The 'copter's ready, sir.'

'Thank you, Harris. There'll be an extremely big bonus in this for you. For all of you.'

'Do you want a guard put on the door here, sir?' asked Harris as the two men walked away from Amber.

'Not necessary. She's not going anywhere. It's twenty-five below out there and she's dressed in silk.'

The guard left, carrying Amber's insulin pouch. Usher leaned down to look into Amber's dazed eyes. 'Goodbye, Amber. It is a shame it had to come to this. Despite what you might think, I like you. I liked your parents too. But business is business.'

Amber lifted her head and tried to spit in his face, but there was no moisture left in her mouth and only a puff of air came out. Daniel Usher sniffed.

'I smell fruit drops. Acetone on your breath. That means you have high acetone levels in your blood. Your body is starting to shut down, Amber. It won't be long now.'

He smiled again, then strode from the room, slamming the outer door behind him. Amber heard a helicopter taking off outside. She wanted to lay her head down on the table again, but she forced herself to stand up. Her only chance was to go after the guard and retrieve her insulin pouch, but first she had to find something warmer than this dress.

She walked around the dining room twice, looking for some curtains to wrap herself in, before she remembered that the building had no windows. For some reason, she found that funny. She began to snort with laughter, but somewhere along the line the laughter turned into a dry sobbing. Amber sank to the floor, ready to give up.

An explosion from the quarry outside brought her back to her senses. As the building rumbled and shook, Amber dragged herself up, using the dining table for support. She stumbled from the dining room and through the next door along the passageway. She walked into a luxuriously decorated living room. There were rich, red, hand-embroidered blankets thrown across the backs of the white sofas. Amber grabbed two of them and wrapped them around her shoulders, one on top of the other. Next, she looked around for something to wrap her feet in. The cushions had tasselled velvet covers. She ripped two of the covers off, wrapped one around each foot and tied the tassels tightly around her insteps and ankles.

She could feel the fog creeping into her head again. Desperately, she headed for the outer door and swung it open. The cold hit her and she stood gasping in the doorway for a few seconds, trying to adjust to the difference in temperature. As she stumbled down the outer steps, all the floodlights in the complex suddenly went out and she could hear men's voices shouting all around her. Too far gone to worry about this turn of events, Amber kept on going. She fell into the snow, got herself up and disappeared around the back of the windowless building.

It was very dark. The cold was making it hard for her to breathe and all her muscles were shuddering in long, painful spasms, but at least the sharp air had cleared her head enough for her to figure out what to do next. She should head for the guardhouse next to the main gate. That was where Harris would have taken her insulin pouch. What she was going to do when she got there, she had no idea. One step at a time was her philosophy right now.

She kept on walking and came up against the mesh

of the perimeter fence. That was good, she thought. If she kept following the fence, it would lead her to the guardhouse. Wrapping her hand in her embroidered blankets, she staggered on through the darkness, trailing her fist along the fence as a guide.

Suddenly the fence ran out. Amber staggered over to the left and fell down into the snow. It was tempting just to lie there, but she picked herself up and pushed on, hands outstretched in front of her, looking for the fence. She did not realize it, but she had just stumbled out through the open main gate of the mine complex.

Head down, she walked a short distance along the rutted snow of the track leading from the mine. Then she fell down, and when she picked herself up again, she was pointing away from the track. Amber stumbled on, trailing her embroidered blankets, and disappeared into the trees to the side of the track.

She kept going for a surprisingly long time, tramping deeper and deeper into the forest as the cold numbed her hands and feet and her body heat dwindled away. Some deep survival instinct was at work and her legs kept moving even though the breath rattled in her lungs and her brain had given up thinking about anything at all.

It was the long, trembling howl of a wolf that penetrated the fog in her head. Amber stopped dead. The howl had been very loud and very close. It had come from the trees directly behind her. She broke into a shambling trot but very quickly ran out of energy and stumbled to a halt again. It was dark in the wood and her sight was beginning to fail, but Amber thought she saw a pale grey shape flickering through the trees like smoke. She turned her head as another shape curved around a spruce trunk and disappeared. Then another, over to her left.

They were all around her.

Amber stood, panting and trembling with exhaustion. She was frightened, but the fear was dull and distant. She was on the edge of consciousness now. Soon, without insulin, she would slip into a coma. Her vision was very blurred, but she thought she could see a lighter patch between the trees. There was a large clearing up ahead. Amber's remaining consciousness became focused on that clearing. She wanted to get out of the wolf-filled darkness beneath the trees. She wanted to see the stars again.

She dragged herself onward, out of the cover of the trees and into the deeper snow of the clearing. There, Amber fell down and found that she could not get to her feet again. She crawled instead, leaving one of her blankets behind at the edge of the clearing. The breath whistled in her throat and the blood roared in her head. When she reached the middle of the clearing, Amber finally gave up. Suddenly, the snow seemed as warm and welcoming as a feather bed. She lay down on the beautifully embroidered red blanket in her white silk dress and closed her tired eyes.

In the shadow of the trees on the edge of the clearing, the wolf pack gathered, padding uncertainly back and forth. There were twelve of them, five males and seven females. They had been tracking a herd of caribou for days and had singled out a pregnant female with an infected hoof. She had been limping along at the back of the herd and falling further and further behind. However, when the pack had finally gone in for the attack, she had found a spurt of energy from somewhere. They had flanked her, nipping at her heels, but she had kept running until she was safely back in the heart of the herd.

The hunt had failed and now the pack was hungry. Very hungry. They had never attacked a human before, but this one was on its own and it was near to death. They paced back and forth on their long legs, whining softly and looking to the alpha male for guidance. He stood on the edge of the clearing, lifting his muzzle to sniff the air. He was a huge wolf. His thick fur was such a pale, silvery grey, it was almost white. His golden eyes stared a challenge at the other males until they stopped their impatient pacing and lowered their heads in submission.

The alpha female, a smaller wolf with darker fur, came to stand alongside him and he nuzzled her affectionately before turning back to survey the clearing. The human was lying motionless in the middle of the clearing but the wolf had lived for a long time and he knew that humans sometimes carried sticks that could hurt from a great distance away. This human would die soon enough. He could smell it. He was prepared to wait a little longer.

Twenty-one

In the windowless living room Alex gazed around him in disbelief as their rescue plan crumbled around them. They had torn through the whole building a second time. Amber was not there.

'We must leave now,' prompted Paulo, listening to the shouts of the guards outside. 'Before they put the floodlights back on.'

Alex groaned. 'Right. We head straight out of the main gate and regroup.'

'Look at this,' said Hex thoughtfully. He pointed to the two cushions that had been dumped on the carpet. 'They're missing their covers. And look. Two of the sofa blankets have been taken. But the rest of the place is immaculate.'

'Hex!' snapped Li. 'This is not the time for a room make-over.'

'Amber took them,' said Hex, thinking hard. 'Why?' His head snapped up and he stared at the others. 'She's already escaped! She's out there somewhere, in sub-zero temperatures, with only a couple of blankets for protection.'

'And no insulin,' said Alex, pulling the pouch with the broken insulin pens from his jacket.

They looked at one another and the dread was clear on their faces.

'Come on,' said Li, running for the door. 'We have to find her.'

They turned out the lights in the passageway and waited for what seemed like an age until their eyes had adjusted to the dark. Then Hex eased open the door and they stepped outside.

'I'll check around the back,' whispered Li, and she disappeared round the corner of the building behind them. Alex, Paulo and Hex moved to the front of the building to check out the positions and numbers of guards by counting torch beams. Alex felt his heart sink as he saw what was happening. What had been a disorganized rabble of men was now an organized force. There was a group clustered around the floodlight generator, another group over at the main gate and, most worrying of all, a whole line of guards was moving slowly across the complex from the far perimeter fence. Their torches wavered back and forth as they carried out a methodical search.

'Right,' whispered Alex. 'We head for the main gate ahead of the search line, looking for Amber as we go. Keep ahead of the torch beams, whatever you do.'

Paulo and Hex nodded and they headed off along the side of the building, hurrying to meet Li at the other end. A second later, they froze as the floodlight generator stuttered into life. The guards had managed to fix the fuel line. With a blinding flash, all the floodlights came on and Paulo, Hex and Alex were caught out in the open with guards all around them.

'There they are!' yelled a guard from the group beside the generator. 'Close in! Close in!'

'Head for the gate!' yelled Alex, as running guards converged on them from all sides.

'Too late,' said Hex. 'They've already closed it.'

Within seconds guards surrounded them and sixteen pistols were levelled at their heads. Alex, Hex and Paulo drew close together, back to back.

'Where's the other one?' asked a stout, older man, stepping forward and throwing back his hood.

'There are no others, Harris,' said Paulo, reading the badge on the man's jacket.

Harris cupped his hands to his mouth and shouted. 'I know you're there somewhere! Come out now, or I shoot one of your friends in the kneecap.'

There was no reply.

Harris drew his pistol and pointed it at Paulo's kneecap.

In her hiding place under the floor of the windowless building, Li watched Paulo turn pale and close his eyes.

'I'm waiting!' called Harris. 'I warn you, I'm not a patient man!'

Li looked desperately from side to side, but she could see no way out of this. Reluctantly, she started to commando-crawl towards the front of the building. Something dug painfully into her hip and her eyes widened as she remembered the pistol she had picked up after her fight with the guard. She reached down and eased it from the pocket of her jacket. Pulling off her outer mitten, she grasped the weapon and released the safety catch. But what to do with it? There were sixteen armed guards out there. She couldn't shoot them all.

'On the count of five!' yelled Harris.

Li began crawling again, heading towards the front of the building. As she did so, the generator that controlled the floodlights came into view.

'One, two . . .' called Harris.

Li frowned at the generator, then her eyes widened as an idea came to her. There was a chance of getting out of this. It was only a chance, but it was better than nothing. Stretching her arms out in front of her and digging her elbows into the ground to steady the pistol, she aimed at the concrete platform under the generator. Closing one eye, she sighted along the barrel of the pistol and began to squeeze the trigger.

'Three, four . . .'

Li pulled the trigger. The bullet smacked into the concrete platform, ricocheted off and hit the metal casing of the generator. The rough concrete and the metal casing acted like flints, sending sparks flying where the bullet hit. The sparks ignited the fuel that had drained from the pipe while it had been disconnected. An instant later, the fuel tank went up with a roar, sending a ball of flame into the sky.

Guards flinched and dropped to the ground as burning fuel and shards of metal flew through the air. One ran off screaming, with the back of his jacket in flames and others hurried to drag him down and roll him in the snow. Li dropped the pistol and crawled out from under the building as, once again, the floodlights went out. Paulo and Hex reached down and grabbed her, lifting her to her feet. They began to run, but already the guards were picking themselves up from the ground.

'Where to now?' screamed Li, her ears still ringing from the report of the pistol.

'Back through the quarry,' shouted Alex, but his heart sank as he saw the distance they had to cover.

The floodlights were out but the whole scene was lit up in the flickering red flames of the burning generator.

'No!' shouted Paulo. 'Head for the helicopter!'

They swerved and ran for the helicopter pad. Before the guards had a chance to react to the sudden change of direction, Paulo had yanked open the door and climbed into the pilot's seat. As the others flung themselves in, he was already flicking switches on the control panel. The helicopter lights came on and the rotors began to turn, quickly increasing in speed until they were a whirring blur. The guards stumbled back, moving away from the deadly rotor blades.

'I didn't know you could fly a helicopter,' shouted Li from the seat beside him.

Paulo hesitated for an instant, wondering how much to say. 'I have taken lessons,' he told her and gave a confident smile.

The truth was, he had completed the first two lessons of a course. He understood the theory of how to fly a helicopter, but all he had actually done was to make the machine rise straight up into the air before setting it down on the ground again.

Paulo placed his feet on the two pedals in the well of the cockpit. They controlled the tail rotor. Next, he grasped a control lever in each hand. He knew that one was called the cyclic and this moved the helicopter forwards, backwards and from side to side. The second lever was called the collective and that controlled the up and down motion as well as the engine speed. So far, so good, thought Paulo. The difficult bit was getting the balance right so that the helicopter flew on an even keel.

'We have to move, Paulo,' said Hex, watching the ground below. Harris was pointing towards them and shouting at two guards. As Hex watched, they stooped and began to run towards the helicopter. Another few seconds and the guards would simply open the door and drag them out. 'Now, Paulo!'

'*Dios*,' muttered Paulo. He moved the collective and the helicopter rose up into the air, leaving the two guards standing on the pad below. Encouraged, Paulo moved the collective the other way and the helicopter fell towards the ground.

'Going down, Paulo!' yelled Hex as the two guards below them dived off the helipad. Hastily, Paulo compensated and they rose again, higher than before. The engine speed increased and the helicopter hovered in place.

'What is this?' demanded Hex. 'A helicopter or an elevator?'

Paulo gingerly pressed down on one of the foot pedals that controlled the tail rotor. Obediently, the helicopter swung round to the left on its axis. Paulo grinned. This was easy! Now all he had to do was make it go forward. He moved the cyclic control and the helicopter nose dived. Guards leaped out of the way as Paulo frantically pulled back on the cyclic. The helicopter straightened up and skimmed along two metres above the ground.

'We need height, Paulo,' said Hex, watching the perimeter fence rush towards them. 'Any time now, Paulo. Paulo!'

At the last second, Paulo swerved the cyclic over to the right and the helicopter banked at such a steep angle, the tips of its rotor blades were centimetres above the ground. Paulo cursed as the helicopter swooped and jerked its way across the complex, sending guards diving for cover.

'Again, the fence, Paulo. The fence!' yelled Hex as the helicopter rushed towards the far fence and the ridge beyond. Paulo cursed again and this time moved both the cyclic and the collective at the same time. The helicopter banked and rose higher in one smooth motion. It skimmed the top of the fence, then turned and headed back over the complex. Paulo adjusted the balance of the controls and the helicopter came to a stop, hovering in mid-air.

'OK, I have it now,' he shouted. 'It is all in the balance.' He eased the cyclic forward and the helicopter began to skim over the complex towards the main gates. They were beginning to hope that they might make it when they saw Harris. He was standing on the helicopter pad with his legs spread and his arms outstretched, aiming his pistol straight at the cockpit of the helicopter.

'Watch out!' yelled Alex.

Just as Harris fired, Paulo swerved and the bullet sang past the side of the cockpit. The helicopter banked steeply and Harris staggered backwards, his mouth open in an O of horror as the scything rotor blades whickered towards him. Everyone in the cockpit felt the jolt as the blades caught Harris across the belly, slicing him badly. Paulo fought to bring the helicopter back under control. Then they were soaring over the main gates of the complex and flying out into the darkness beyond.

For a moment there was a shocked silence in the cockpit. Paulo struggled to keep his stomach contents in place as he guided the helicopter away from the mine. Their searchlight skimmed across the forest below, picking out tree tops in its white circle of light.

'That poor man,' said Alex grimly.

'"That poor man" was about to shoot us down,' protested Hex, but there was no real anger in his voice. 'Forget him. I'm more interested in how we find Amber. She's out there somewhere, without . . .' His voice roughened and he stopped without finishing his sentence.

'I spotted her tracks in the snow when I went round the back of the building,' said Li. 'They went round the perimeter fence, out of the gates and into the woods on the right-hand side.'

They all looked down at the countless trees rushing

past in the searchlight beam. It seemed an impossible task to find one girl in all that, but they had to try. Amber's life depended on them.

'Wait a minute,' said Alex. 'If she walked out of the gates, it must have been after I opened them, while the floodlights were still down. We saw Usher leave the building as we waited to move in, so she can't have escaped before that.'

There was a short silence as Alpha Force looked at one another, realizing that they had only just missed Amber. She must have been stumbling out of the main gates under cover of darkness as they searched the building she had just left.

'How long has she been out there?' asked Hex.

Alex looked at his watch and was astonished to see that, although it felt as though hours had gone by since he had opened the main gates, only fifteen minutes had passed. 'Fifteen minutes,' he said. 'She can't have got far. Especially in the state she must be in.'

'All right,' said Hex. 'We have a rough location and we have a timescale. That narrows it down a lot.'

Paulo banked the helicopter and came down low over the trees. 'Let us start looking,' he said.

Twenty-two

In the woods behind the quarry, Ice was lying at the head of the team, with his nose and paws curled under his tail and his head resting on one of Amber's mittens. Suddenly his head came up and he gazed out into the darkness. His ears were cocked, his blue eyes were intensely concentrated and his nose was twitching, sniffing the night air.

He had caught a familiar scent. It was the same scent that was slowly fading from the mitten at his feet. Ice leaped up and tried to run towards the scent but he was yanked back by his tugline. With a snarl, he turned on the other sleeping dogs, harrying and nipping them to their feet. Once again Ice tried to run towards the scent. Again, his tugline pulled him back. The third time he tried, the other dogs caught his urgency and began pulling too, leaning into their harnesses. Their claws raked the snow and they yelped with excitement.

Frodo began to dig around the snow-hook that was anchoring the middle of the gangline to the ground. Donald joined in. The snow-hook loosened, then jerked out of the ground. The middle section of the gangline sprang free and, for the fourth time, Ice tried to lead the team in the direction of the scent. Again they were pulled back. The brake at the back of the sled was still digging firmly into the ground. The team came to a halt, panting with exertion, then Ice's head came up and his nose twitched again.

The scent was still there on the wind, but another scent had joined it. The wild, rank smell of wolf. Ice wrinkled his muzzle in a snarl as he threw his whole weight behind the harness. The other dogs joined in and, slowly, the spring-loaded sled brake was bent out of shape until it sprang back out of the snow. Ice and his team flattened out and raced towards the two scents, the empty sled bouncing along behind them.

In the middle of the clearing, Amber lay motionless on her red blanket as the high blood sugar levels in her body pulled her deeper into unconsciousness. Her eyes were half-closed and her breathing was shallow. She had the beginnings of frostbite in her toes and her core temperature was very low, but the blanket was insulating her from the frozen ground beneath her and slowing the onset of hypothermia.

She had been lying motionless for five minutes now, and the wolves at the edge of the clearing were becoming bolder. The alpha female looked from Amber to the alpha male and then back to Amber. Her meaning was clear. The big, silver-furred male looked at his mate, then finally stepped out of the shelter of the trees and began to lope across the clearing towards Amber. The other wolves fanned out around him, falling instinctively into the pincer formation they used when hunting.

Ice pulled his lips back in a snarl. The scent of wolf was overwhelming now. He could smell many of them, males and females, and they were very close. He raced along the forest trail with the other dogs at his heels. The trees were thinning out here, and there was a lighter patch up ahead. Ice redoubled his efforts and, suddenly, the team burst out into a clearing lit by the rising moon.

The wolves were there, spread out across the area in a semicircle. They were slinking towards a body lying in the snow. Ice roared as he pelted towards them with the team behind him. The wolves jumped and some of the more timid ones fell back to stand behind the alpha male.

The silver wolf stood over Amber and turned to face Ice. His golden eyes were blazing and the hackles along his back were raised, making him look even bigger than he was, but Ice kept on coming without the slightest hesitation. The silver wolf might beat him for size, but Ice was full of a cold hatred. He launched himself into the air and the wolf leaped over Amber's body towards him. They met in a fury of snapping jaws, came down in the snow, then rolled as the rest of the dog team cannoned into them.

The team managed to come to a halt and Ice

sprang to his feet again, but the silver wolf was faster. He pounced, knocking him to the ground. Ice became hopelessly tangled in the gangline and, as he struggled to get to his feet again, the wolf moved in for the kill. Jaws wide, he went for his throat, but an instant later the wolf and Ice were both knocked sideways as the sled finished swinging round in a wide arc and smacked into them.

The silver wolf scrambled to his feet and jumped backwards, away from the sled. For the first time, the big animal hesitated. The sled had come to a stop on its side a couple of metres away and it smelled wrong to the wolf. It smelled of humans and plastic and other unnatural things. Ice was still hopelessly entangled in the gangline and his belly was exposed. The silver wolf could have ripped it open with one slash, but the sled was there, right next to Ice, and the sled was wrong. The wolf took another step back on his long legs and Ice managed to scramble to his feet again.

Then the dark alpha female moved up alongside the silver wolf and his confidence returned. Together, they moved in on Ice, and the other wolves moved in on the rest of the team. They took their time, working together almost telepathically as each pack member selected a target and teamed up in pairs to attack the bigger dogs. The dogs stood their ground around Amber and snarled bravely, but they were smaller than the wolves and they were outnumbered seven to twelve. Added to that, the wolves had complete freedom of movement and the dogs were harnessed to the gangline.

At a signal from the alpha wolf, the pack moved in for the attack and the dogs disappeared beneath an avalanche of grey fur and teeth and claws. But barely seconds later, the wolf pack exploded outwards across the clearing and raced into the trees as a whirlwind of light and noise came roaring over the tree tops.

'How long has she been out there now?' asked Li, as the helicopter quartered another square of forest.

'Twenty-five minutes,' said Alex, after glancing at his watch.

There was a short silence as they all tried to imagine how long an inadequately dressed person could survive in sub-zero temperatures.

'At least she's in the trees,' said Li. 'The trees will protect her from the wind.'

'Perhaps we should search another part of the forest,' suggested Paulo.

'No,' said Hex. 'She must be somewhere within this square. She has to be. Double back, Paulo. We do one more sweep.'

Paulo headed back over the square of forest and they all stared intently from their windows.

'There!' cried Li, suddenly sitting bolt upright in her seat. 'There was something down there!'

She had caught a flash of red and a whirling mass of grey in the searchlight beam as it panned across the ground below.

'Turn back, Paulo! There was something down there!'

Paulo banked the helicopter and this time the searchlight picked out a pack of grey shapes streaking across the snow.

'Wolves!' shouted Hex.

Alex looked from the other window and spotted Amber, lying on a scarlet blanket in the snow. 'There she is!' he called. 'Amber's down there!'

'And the sled and the team,' said Li. 'How on earth did they get there?'

Paulo lined up the big helicopter above the clearing and began to ease it down. He had managed this easily during his lesson but that had been in daylight on a helicopter pad. This was in darkness and snow was whirling all around them, stirred up by the rotors. Paulo was having trouble judging where the ground was.

'Come on, Paulo!' yelled Hex.

Paulo eased the helicopter down another metre and they hit the ground hard with a bone-shaking jolt. As soon as they were sure the helicopter was going to stay down, Hex, Li and Alex jumped out and ran, crouching until they were out of range of the rotors. Paulo turned off the engine and jumped out after them while the rotors were still spinning.

They reached Amber and fell on their knees beside her. She was cold and still. Hex put his cheek to her mouth to feel for any trace of breath and a look of immeasurable relief crossed his face. 'She's still alive.'

Paulo grabbed an insulin pen from his inside jacket pocket and jammed it into Amber's thigh. He pressed the button on the top of the pen and the life-saving dose of insulin was punched through Amber's skin.

'Now we must warm her up,' said Alex.

Together, Paulo and Hex lifted Amber on the blanket and lowered her gently on to the sled. Li untangled the gangline, noting that some of the dogs were bleeding from torn ears or ripped muzzles.

'You know, I think they fought the wolves to save Amber,' she said, as she led the dogs towards the trees.

'Let's hope we can do the same,' said Hex, trotting alongside the sled and never taking his eyes off Amber.

Once they had found a sheltered spot, Alpha Force moved into action. Hex ran to collect dry wood, Alex instructed Paulo to dig in the snow under the trees until he had found half a dozen smooth, oval stones, Li dressed Amber in her arctic clothes, which were still on the sled, and Alex put Amber's feet to warm against his chest, under his layers of jackets and fleeces. Their iciness made him gasp and shiver, but it was essential to start the warming process to avoid more severe frostbite.

Once the fire was going, Alex instructed Paulo to put the stones to warm beside it, then collect everyone's inner gloves and pop a heated stone into each of them.

'We must warm her blood,' explained Alex, his face twisting against the bitter taste as he chewed on a couple of painkillers. 'The warmed blood will circulate and heat the rest of her body.' Carefully, Paulo slipped the wrapped stones under Amber's clothes, putting them in all the places where the blood flowed close to the surface. 'That's good,' said Alex. 'One on the back of her neck, one in each armpit, one in the pit of the stomach and one in the small of her back.'

Paulo sat back and looked at Alex, who nodded in satisfaction. Amber was lying on the reflective foil bag from Alex's survival tin and Ice was lying alongside her on the sled, adding his body warmth to the equation. The fire was burning well and Hex had built up a reflective bank of snow to maximize the warmth. Li had melted two billycans of snow and was bringing them to the boil, ready to make a hot drink with the stock cubes from Alex's survival pouch, and Alex was still warming Amber's feet on his stomach.

'That's good,' said Alex.

Li took one of the billycans, added some potassium permanganate to the water, and carried it over to the dogs. Then she used a wadded piece of bandage from the medical kit to bathe the dogs' wounds. Ice seemed to be unscathed, but Frodo had a nasty rip in one of his big, pointed ears. He whined as Li bathed it and she soothed him gently. Stinker had a flap of skin hanging loose at the side of his mouth and Beauty had a gash across her muzzle.

'Don't worry,' whispered Li as Beauty looked up at her with big, dark eyes. 'You won't have a scar.'

She moved on, checking the other dogs, while Hex came up to sit beside Amber.

'Did we find her in time?' he asked, pushing Amber's hands under his jacket to warm them. 'Did she get the insulin in time?'

Paulo frowned, staring at Amber's still face. 'I do not know,' he said truthfully.

'Is there anything else we can do?' asked Li.

'We must wait,' said Paulo. 'Only wait.'

TWENTY-THREE

Tap, tap, tap, tap-tap, tap.

Amber frowned and opened her eyes. Hex was sitting right next to her head, tapping away at his palmtop keyboard.

'Whassalla noise about?' she mumbled.

Hex stopped tapping and turned to her with a huge and delighted smile on his face. 'Hey, Amber,' he said softly. 'Welcome back.'

Amber scowled, which seemed to delight Hex even more.

'That close, was I?' she said, watching his face.

Hex quickly rearranged his face into his usual world-weary expression. 'Sorry. No death-bed scenes. You're going to live to write a book about it. *Trekking the Arctic in a Dinner Dress*.'

Amber smiled, then found her scowl again. 'I said—'

'"Whassalla noise about." I heard you,' said Hex. 'I'm making you a present.'

'What is it?'

'I'll show you when it's ready,' said Hex.

Amber turned her head away in irritation and came nose to nose with Ice, who panted happily and licked her face. 'Yeuch. Dog breath,' muttered Amber.

'Don't insult Ice,' said Li, sitting on the edge of the sled and smiling down at Amber. 'He saved your life. He fought wolves for you. Do you remember?'

'I remember the wolves,' shuddered Amber. She reached out a gloved hand and buried her fingers in Ice's fur.

'Are you cold still?' asked Paulo, bending over her.

'Nope. I'm warm enough. But I feel pretty bad,' said Amber. 'My head aches. My muscles feel like putty.'

'They are the after-effects of hyperglycaemia—'

'Duh! I know! How long have I been out?'

'It is three hours since I injected the insulin,' said Paulo.

Amber nodded, then winced as she became aware of the throbbing pain in her toes. 'My feet hurt,' she said.

'Don't worry,' said Alex, from the bottom of the sled. 'It's not serious. Frostnip rather than frostbite. It'll hurt for a while, but you're not going to lose any toes.'

'Alex has been acting as your human hot-water bottle,' explained Li.

Amber lifted her head and gazed down at Alex. 'Thanks.'

'No problem. It's about all I could do, with this injured shoulder.'

Amber winced again as her stomach clenched with hunger pangs. 'I need food,' she said.

'And soon you shall have some,' said Hex. 'I've been in touch with Amaruk. He's on his way to us right now. He says they're preparing a meal for us back in the village.'

'Good,' said Amber, and a mischievous glint came into her eyes. 'Alex hasn't tried the Inuit ice cream yet.'

'Is it good?' asked Alex.

'You are in for a treat,' promised Paulo.

'What about Boomer?' asked Amber, becoming serious again. 'Did Amaruk say anything about Boomer?'

'He's going to be fine,' said Hex. 'Kikik stitched him up and he's lying in state in front of the stove in their kitchen. Amaruk asked about your shoulder, Alex.'

'It's fine,' said Alex, but his face was drawn with pain.

'And now, my present,' said Hex. 'Watch this.'

He turned the screen of his palmtop towards Amber and pressed a button. Amber watched in fascinated horror as an edited version of Hex's camcorder footage played on the small screen, complete with subtitles. She saw Papaluk lying in the snow like a glittering ice princess, with the caption 'Daniel Usher killed this woman'. Next, she saw her own frightened face as a man held a sawn-off shotgun to her head. 'Daniel Usher tried to kill this girl', read the caption.

Amber watched as images of cyanide waste pouring into the shaft at the Usher mine were spliced with images of an Inuit woman cradling her sick baby. 'Usher Mines poisoned this baby', read the caption.

'It's good,' she began, then drew a shocked breath as a photograph of her own parents smiled out at her from the screen.

'Where did you get that?' she asked.

'Downloaded it from the Net,' said Hex. 'And this too,' he added, as the screen showed footage of the dam project Amber's parents had been trying to stop.

'What are you going to do with it?' asked Amber.

'Aha. Now comes the good part,' grinned Hex, glancing at his watch. It was nearly time.

He pulled the mobile phone from his pocket and keyed in a number.

'Who're you calling?' asked Amber.

Hex held up a hand. 'Hi, Gina,' he said, and suddenly he was a New York businessman with a crisp, authoritative voice. 'Ross here, from Daniel's

New York office. Yes, I know he's about to go on air. That's why I'm calling. I have the new footage here.'

Hex winked at Amber as he listened to Gina. 'Well, I'm telling you now. Daniel wants this new footage playing behind him as he makes his broadcast, not the footage you already have.'

Hex listened again. They could all hear Gina's panicked voice squawking up the register. 'Gina,' he interrupted, 'do you want to have a job at the end of this broadcast? Then play the new footage. Good. Thank you.'

Hex held the phone to his ear with one shoulder while he reached for his palmtop and began keying in the information Gina gave him. 'OK, Gina, I'm sending it to you now. It's all edited and ready. Just patch it straight in.'

'Oh, man!' grinned Amber, as Hex ended the call. 'I wish I could see it.'

'You can,' said Hex. He tapped instructions into the palmtop and they all gathered round as Daniel Usher's live broadcast appeared on the screen.

'Shouldn't you contact the police, too?' asked Amber, as Usher appeared onscreen.

'Already have,' whispered Hex. 'And the press. They should be arriving just about when his broadcast finishes. I couldn't let him miss his moment of glory.'

As Daniel Usher smiled out from the screen, he looked the very image of a decent, successful man. His suit fitted him perfectly. The grey wings of hair at his temples only made him more distinguished and his blue eyes were frank and open.

'What a dangerous man,' muttered Paulo, gazing at the handsome face.

'Here we go!' crowed Amber as the big screen in the studio flickered into life. As Usher talked about his commitment to the environment and making things better, Hex's footage began to roll behind him.

'How many people are seeing this?' asked Alex.

'Prime time evening television?' smiled Hex. 'Millions.'

'Good,' said Li. 'Oh, look! He's realizing something's up . . .'

Daniel Usher stopped talking and stood up from behind the desk as a young woman with a head mike and a clipboard hurried on and whispered in his ear.

'Hello, Gina,' grinned Hex in his New York accent.

Usher turned to look at the screen behind him, then turned back to camera. His face was brick-red with fury and his blue eyes glared out from the screen. Gina was pointing off-camera. Daniel Usher's face changed again as he tried to assume an air of authority once more, but the two police officers coming up on either side of him were not impressed.

Alpha Force cheered as the police marched Usher out of the studio.

'Look!' laughed Alex. 'The camera's following! Even his own television company's turned against him.'

'He's just another criminal in the news, now,' drawled Hex, with a satisfied smile on his face.

Alpha Force watched as Daniel Usher walked out into a familiar scene of popping flashbulbs and strobing police car lights but then, suddenly, the little screen went blank.

'Blast!' muttered Hex, grabbing the palmtop. 'We lost the connection with the satellite. How did that happen?'

'I think we have interference,' said Paulo, pointing at the sky.

They all looked up. 'Oh,' breathed Amber. A curtain of shimmering light was pulsing across the dark sky above the trees. As they watched, the colours flickered, changing from green to violet to gold and back again.

'The northern lights,' smiled Alex. 'Amazing.'

'Nothing amazing about them,' grunted Hex, still disgusted that the atmospheric interference had cut short his television show. 'Streams of charged protons and electrons hitting particles of gas in the upper atmosphere, that's all they are—'

'Shut up, Hex,' said Amber. 'And listen. You can hear them.'

Hex subsided and they listened as a faint, faraway sound, like the ringing of thousands of tiny bells, sounded in the air.

'Remember what Papaluk said about the northern lights?' asked Paulo, smiling down at Li. 'Spirit torches, held by the people we love, come to lead us home.'

Li nodded and gazed up at the shimmering ribbons of light. She leaned back against Paulo's chest and the colours danced across her face as, finally, she cried for her friend Papaluk, who had walked upon the land.

'Hello, Mom; hello, Dad,' said Amber softly. 'If you can hear me, I just want to say, I'm doing fine. Really, I am. And, well, we got him for you.' She eased herself up on the sled as a thought occurred to her. 'Guys? Remember when we first met?'

'Who could forget it?' said Alex, thinking of those first, tense days of squabbling on the sail-training ship.

'You were so angry at the world,' said Paulo. 'You were wearing your parents' wedding rings around your neck in an Omega sign.'

'Omega. The end,' said Amber. 'It seemed like the end to me then. But – not to get too mushy here – we made a new beginning with Alpha Force. And now . . . Now I feel as though we've come full circle. We caught the guy who killed my parents. So . . .' Amber hesitated, gazing around at the others. 'So, have we reached another end? Should we, you know, disband Alpha Force?'

'Do you want us to disband?' asked Alex, looking at Amber.

'Hell, no!' said Amber. 'But it gets a bit dangerous at times—'

'Understatement alert!' cried Li.

'—and I just want to make sure you guys want to stay on board. You know, if you wanted to call it a day . . .'

'And leave all this behind?' said Hex, spreading his arms to take in their filthy, battered state.

'We cannot disband,' said Paulo. 'We have a new recruit.' He reached out and ruffled Ice's fur, then hastily withdrew his hand as the big dog sat up and looked at him coldly.

Alex felt a thrill of dread run through him at the thought of losing the rest of Alpha Force. 'I'm not going anywhere,' he said firmly.

'Sorry, Amber. You're stuck with me for life,' said Li.

'It's unanimous,' said Hex. 'Alpha Force is here to stay. Happy now?'

'No big deal,' said Amber, settling back on the sled with a sigh of relief. 'Just checking.'

CHRIS RYAN'S TOP TEN TIPS FOR SURVIVAL IN CAVE SYSTEMS

Alpha Force travel through underwater tunnels up near the Arctic Circle, but there are many different types of cave system in the world. They can be horizontal, vertical, flooded, dry, hot, cold, humid, draughty, muddy, sandy . . . sometimes several of these features can be found in one single cave! They all have one thing in common, though – exploring them means going underground into natural tunnels and caverns in the earth's rock.

Man may have once lived in caves, but you should treat any expedition into caves or tunnels with great respect. Every year, all over the world, cave rescue authorities have to deal with people who have gone underground without adequate preparation or equipment. Don't be one of them! Many caving trips are carried out every weekend all over the world with people enjoying a safe and fun time. Proper training and common sense go a long way. If caving is something that interests you, why not ask your library if there are any local clubs you could join to learn the basic skills and techniques?

1. Planning

First and foremost, do plan ahead. Many of the big cave systems have maps available and these should be studied in advance and stored carefully (in water-proof bags or covers). My advice to you is to stay clear of any caves that are prone to flooding because cave diving is one of the most dangerous sports known to man. Make sure you find out in advance if the tunnels do flood and, if so, when. For example, you could discover that some tunnels close to the water are flooded during the period of high tide, so you will be fine in the system if you can just sit tight until the tide falls again. Or perhaps the tunnels will be flooded if there is heavy rain, so check out the weather forecast, not only to find out if it's going to rain, but also if it recently *has* rained, as this can cause a flash-flood effect that could happen hours – even a day – after heavy rain. You'll need more than an umbrella to survive a downpour if you're stuck in a tunnel with the water rising fast! It can be extremely fierce and dangerous, powering through the tunnels like an express train and taking everything with it.

Make sure you tell someone responsible what your plans are. Tell them your route, your planned time underground and any essential medical facts (e.g. if one of you is diabetic, like Amber), so that if you don't return on time, someone will know and a search party can be sent out, armed with all the necessary information to find you. Never even consider going underground on your own. If you should have an accident, your chances of survival are very slim and you might well even put others' lives at risk as they try to find you.

In the SAS, advance planning is always key to the success of an operation. Time taken in preparation can save lives, so don't skip it.

2. Equipment

Underground caving requires varied specialized equipment, depending upon the kind of system. Alpha Force know that they are going through tunnels flooded with freezing water, and wear vulcanized rubber dry suits and full face masks.

An absolute minimum of equipment I would want with me if going into any cave system would include:

- ropes: to rope yourselves together and, if necessary, for climbing down steep slopes. One of approximately five metres in length each should be sufficient
- a beta light: a light-emitting crystal about the size of a small coin. It's expensive, but everlasting and I've found it invaluable in the past. Alex always carries one in his survival kit.
- a torch *and* a spare, stored in waterproof containers.

- chalk, again stored in a waterproof container
- a watch with a luminous face and waterproof casing; this is essential if you need to keep an eye on the timing of something like a high tide
- a compass: the type with luminous buttons
- protection for your head, preferably a caver's helmet with a light fixed on it, so your hands are free
- first-aid kit for essential injuries: include bandages, plasters, aspirin and water-sterilizing tablets
- waterproof outerwear
- thermal underwear! Yes, I know it sounds like something your granny would tell you, but thermals can be a real life-saver in a cold, dark cave if you have to stay there overnight!

3. Don't panic

Underground in the dark, in a tunnel that is only as high as your body when you lie face-down on the ground, with a huge amount of rock above you, it is very easy to feel claustrophobic – and claustrophobia can turn easily into panic. Panic helps no-one and you could injure yourself and lose or damage vital equipment. If, like Hex, you feel yourself beginning to feel claustrophobic or panicky, try and slow yourself down, breathe as calmly as possible and focus on something very specific to take your mind off the general situation. And remember – claustrophobia is no joke, so don't try and spook others with you if you feel OK yourself.

When I was in Belize, a number of guys from our boat troop who were qualified divers took me into the jungle to dive the blue hole – this links a large cave system that comes out into the sea. We swam in there with air tanks for approximately one hour and it was very claustrophobic and cramped. It took all my strength and concentration not to panic. I just kept getting reassurance from the other guys who were trained divers.

A positive mental attitude – much easier if you know you have the skills and knowledge to survive – can also really help here. Even if everyone else in your group is feeling scared and negative, you can make a big difference if you remain calm and confident.

4. Don't get lost

Getting lost is the biggest danger underground. It's very difficult to keep any idea of direction when tunnels turn very gently and, in the dark, you can easily miss openings in the rock. Ideally, try and retrace your steps to your original entrance, and mark any turns or forks very clearly from the moment you enter the system. You can use chalk-marks, piles of pebbles or both, but make the signs very clear and understandable. This will also help any rescuer who follows you. If possible, have one person check each side of any tunnel as you move slowly along it, and it can be a good idea to rope everyone together. That way, you can't get separated and no-one can fall down a hole either!

If squeezing through small gaps do remember that you should turn round if you want to go back. If you try to move backwards, you could get clothing or equipment stuck on projecting rock.

If you have to travel through a system, use your compass to make sure you keep heading in the direction you want. It's possible to wander round and round in circles in a forest: you can easily do the same underground. In some caves, the rock formations have a high metal content which can affect your compass bearing so it is very important to constantly check your compass in case it is being pulled off.

One tip: check the cave walls regularly for any signs of water-marks. An underground river could partially flood some of the tunnels and your marks would be washed away.

5. Dealing with injuries

If you've ever banged your knee on a rock, you'll know how unforgiving rock is. You are likely to suffer bruises, cuts and scrapes underground – and watch your head for low-hanging bumps (that's why you should wear a helmet). With an uneven surface, falls are also possible and either you, or a friend, could be unlucky enough to break a bone if you fall awkwardly.

If a limb is broken, it will need to be immobilized so that no further movement makes it worse. The best way to do this is by strapping it to a splint. You could make one of these from anything available – a piece of wood, a branch, even a roll of newspaper. Put something soft between the splint and the limb and make sure it's not too tight – you don't want to cut off the blood supply. If no splint is available, you could strap the limb to the person's body or another uninjured limb – e.g. strap both legs together. Obviously, if someone has broken a bone in their leg and you've then strapped their legs together, they won't be able to walk any further so you may then need to improvise a stretcher to carry the person with you. If possible, in these circumstances, designate someone as the advance scout and let them go ahead (carefully and making sure they don't pass any forks or turns) to check the route before you all move off as a group, carrying the injured person.

It really is worthwhile getting some first-aid skills if you are likely to travel in any dangerous areas. Every serving soldier in the SAS is trained in basic first aid and we carry essential basic treatments with us on all operations. During my career in the SAS, I was a trained medic and I was constantly treating colleagues who had been injured. It is an invaluable skill which will be called upon when training in arduous conditions. Another commitment we had was a project called *Hearts and Minds*: we would travel into remote areas and give medical help to the indigenous people. Why not ask at your school or library and find out if there are any first-aid courses you can take in your area?

6. Light

It's virtually impossible to move about underground without light and no experienced caver would dream of exploring without a helmet with a light on it – and spare batteries. Without light, you really will be in deep trouble! A beta light will also help with map-reading. Tread carefully – caves and tunnels can have uneven surfaces, sudden holes or loose, shingly ground that slopes away suddenly.

If stopping for a rest, try and save the light by turning all but one off – you want your batteries to last as long as possible. And watch for outside light entering the system; it could signal your way out.

7. Air

The air within cave systems can be musty and damp, depending on how far you are from the open. It is also a good indicator of where there are openings to the outside. Cool air usually blows into a cave, so use your noses and try to follow the air to find an escape route.

8. Water

Many cave systems have underground springs, but it is still a good idea to use water-sterilizing tablets before drinking any of the water. In any survival situation, finding freshwater is a number one priority – you can only last about three days without water. If you find a source of drinkable water, make sure you mark it clearly on any map you have – and check you can find your way back to it if necessary.

9. Safety when swimming or diving into underwater cave systems

Alpha Force are in the Arctic area to train – but also to have fun, which is why they take diving equipment with them on their trip into the interior. They hoped to do some ice-diving – an extreme sport where a hole is cut in the ice of a frozen lake and you then dive underneath it.

You could run across short sections of flooded tunnels, but swimming through cave systems is really only for experienced cavers who have trained properly. In any cave system, however, you could discover underground rivers or pools. These are likely to be very cold (no sun), so do take care. Ice-cold water can be a killer. If you should fall into cold water – especially through ice – it will literally take the breath out of you. Your body will curl up, you won't be able to use your muscles and you'll be shivering. If you can't get out, you could die in 15–20 minutes. In the Arctic region, where Alpha Force were operating, the sub-zero temperature would kill someone who fell in within minutes! However, the body shuts down so revival is possible after a longer period than normal. If you have to pull an unconscious companion out of cold water and they seem to be dead, do still try artificial respiration as you warm them up (or while you wait for the emergency services to arrive, if possible) as they could still survive. One doctor, an expert in reviving people, has said: 'They're not dead until they're warm and dead.'

10. Signal for rescue

A mobile phone will be useless underground but it is still possible to do as much as possible to help rescuers.

Mark your route clearly and, if possible, leave notes in waterproof bags to let rescuers know the number in your party, any injuries, the time you passed etc.

If you find an exit coming out high on a cliff, a fire can produce smoke and attract attention.

BE SAFE!

Chris Ryan

Random House Children's Books and Chris Ryan would like to make it clear that these tips are for use in a serious situation only, where your life may be at risk. We cannot accept any liability for inappropriate usage in normal conditions.

About the Author

Chris Ryan joined the SAS in 1984 and has been involved in numerous operations with the regiment. During the Gulf War, he was the only member of an eight-man team to escape from Iraq, three colleagues being killed and four captured. It was the longest escape and evasion in the history of the SAS. For this he was awarded the Military Medal. He wrote about his remarkable escape in the adult bestseller *The One That Got Away* (1995), which was also adapted for screen.

He left the SAS in 1994 and is now the author of a number of bestselling thrillers for adults. His work in security takes him around the world and he has also appeared in a number of television series, most recently *Hunting Chris Ryan*, in which his escape and evasion skills were demonstrated to the max. The *Alpha Force* titles are his first books for young readers.

If you enjoyed this book look out for others in the series:

ALPHA FORCE

Target: Drug Rat

RAT-CATCHER

Alpha Force are an elite team of five highly-skilled individuals brought together to battle injustice. Together they join a covert SAS operation in South America, fighting to catch an evil drugs baron. To gain information, they infiltrate a tight-knit community of street kids then head into the isolated mountains where a terrifying and twisted hunt is to test their individual skills to the max . . .

ISBN 0 099 43925 5

If you enjoyed this book look out for others in the series:

ALPHA FORCE

Target: Child-Slavers

DESERT PURSUIT

Alpha Force are a unique group of five individuals, each with special skills, each ready to go anywhere in the world to help others in need. Undercover, they head for the Sahara Desert, resolved to gather evidence of young landmine victims. But they are catapulted into a desperate race across the desert when they discover a terrible evil – a gang of child-slavers operating in the area.

The team is in pursuit . . .

ISBN 0 099 43926 3